THE
EMERALD
DAGGER

ALSO BY DENNIS STAGINNUS:

The Raiders of Folklore: Book One
The Eye of Odin

THE RAIDERS OF FOLKLORE

THE EMERALD DAGGER

DENNIS STAGINNUS

STAG'S HEAD BOOKS

The Emerald Dagger
The Raiders of Folklore – Book 2
Copyright © 2016 Stag's Head Books

This book is a work of fiction. Names, characters, places, and events in this book are either products of the author's imagination or are used fictitiously. Any resemblance to actual events, places, or persons living or dead, is purely coincidental.

Published by Stag's Head Books

Cover Design: Pintado
Illustrations: Jennifer Pendergast
Book Design: Maureen Cutajar

Visit the author's website at:
www.dennisstaginnus.com

ISBN 978-0-9936824-8-3

This is for you, Mom and Dad.
Thank you for always believing in me.

Prologue

The serpent was five times larger than Halfdan expected. It slithered between stone pillars, scaly skin glistening in the deep amber torchlight. The Viking fought to keep his breathing steady. He watched the viper twine along the far side of the tomb. Its forked tongue flicked, searching for his scent.

Apart from its size, Halfdan was under no illusion the creature was an ordinary snake. It didn't react like any typical reptile he'd encountered before. It could reason. Plan.

The last hour had been proof of that.

Halfdan's escape from the tomb's twisting tunnels had been more dangerous than expected. After stashing another fragment of Mimir's Stone, the creature hunted them on their return trip to the surface, killing most of his men in the process. It prowled the darkness like a skulking worm, snatching and coiling around each Varangian. Halfdan remembered their screams, the sounds of their crunching bones as the snake squeezed them like ripe grapes.

1

Twenty had entered the Serpent's Tomb. Now only he and two others remained.

Halfdan whistled lightly. He made eye contact with Solveig, who was hiding behind the opposite pillar. With a single look, Halfdan knew the other man's thoughts: *What do we do?*

He answered with hand signals. *Kill it.*

Not sure we can, Solveig gestured back.

Halfdan nodded and pointed to the tomb's entrance. *Escape?*

Solveig agreed enthusiastically. *You distract. I'll make for the exit.*

Halfdan rolled his eyes. *Of course, you veslingr, make me do the dangerous work.*

The other Viking flashed a mischievous grin.

The two had been boyhood friends, serving on raiding parties together since they were fourteen. They'd been inseparable, saved each other's lives countless times, and plundered enough monasteries to collect a lifetime of riches. But no treasure compared to that of the Eye of Odin. Despite its worth, their discovery of the powerful artifact had become a curse. A prize they could neither use nor sell, but one that held the fate of countless lives.

Solveig's grin faltered. He stuck his chin out toward the farthest pillar. *What about Astrid?* The witch's trembling shoulder poked out from behind the column. *Can she make it?*

Halfdan shrugged and peeked to his left. The tomb's entrance was only twenty faomrs away. He nodded back. *We can make it.*

At that moment, the rattle at the end of the serpent's tail vibrated, sending an eerie warning through the tomb: Just try to escape my nest.

It wants to flush us out, Halfdan thought grimly. *It's waiting for us to make our move.*

No matter. They had to get out of there.

On five, Solveig gestured.

Halfdan swallowed and gave him the thumbs up.

The other Viking held up his fingers.

Five—four—

Halfdan readied himself, bobbing up and down in rhythm with Solveig's counting.

Three—two—

He gripped his sword with both hands.

One.

Halfdan set his jaw and jumped from his hiding spot. "Here!" he shouted. His voice echoed off the tomb walls. "Here I am, you confounded *slange!*"

The serpent's head jerked in his direction. It rose like a cobra, revealing its pale underbelly.

"What are you waiting for? Come and get me!"

Like a tube of armored muscle, the snake rocketed forward. Its bulk knocked into pillars, shaking dust loose from the ceiling.

Halfdan dashed between columns and jumped over fallen statues of Roman emperors. He reached the place where the witch sat, paralyzed with fear.

"Astrid. Follow me," he yelled, holding out his hand.

The girl refused to move.

"Astrid!"

She remained motionless, back pressed against the stone pillar, staring into empty space.

Halfdan glanced toward Solveig. His friend rushed from one pillar to the next, already making his way to the tomb's exit.

"I don't have time for this."

Halfdan grabbed the witch's limp arm and yanked her to her feet. He was about to drag her after him when the serpent's barrel-shaped body blocked their path.

Unblinking, reptilian eyes stared down at them.

Halfdan stood there, transfixed. Every one of his senses became hyper-aware. In that moment, there was only him and the serpent: the beast's head, its overlapping scales, its interlocking rings vibrating a hypnotic chant. Its saber-like fangs.

The snake lashed out like a cracking whip.

Halfdan swung his sword. The blade bounced harmlessly off the creature's scales. The viper struck again. This time, Halfdan managed to slash its mouth. The snake jerked back, thrashing out with its tail instead. Halfdan ducked and rolled. The wayward strike smashed into a pillar. The column disintegrated, sending chunks of carved stone crashing to the floor.

From the corner of his eye, he caught a sliver of light begin to shrink. Solveig had made it to the entrance. He was closing the tomb door.

Halfdan cursed. Astrid was dead weight. She would only slow him down if they dashed for the exit.

In a split-second decision, Halfdan shoved the comatose witch toward the roiling serpent. He turned and sprinted away. The witch's ear-piercing scream shrieked behind him.

Better her than me, he thought. But would the delay be enough?

Scraping sounds, like a thousand knives grinding on stone, warned him the serpent was in pursuit. He didn't dare look back. The thought of his body being constricted until his bones shattered willed his legs to pump faster. He jumped over more toppled statues and dodged chunks of fallen pillar. The tomb's entrance grew tantalizingly close. He felt a pang of fear, thinking the serpent would snatch him right at the last second, inches from freedom.

Reaching the door, Halfdan squeezed through the gap and tripped onto a narrow outcropping. Solveig heaved the tomb door shut behind him.

Halfdan lay on the ground, gasping for breath. "We did it," he said, feeling the burden lift from his soul. Another runestone fragment had been hidden away.

"Unfortunate that Astrid did not make it." Solveig smiled and offered his friend a hand up.

Halfdan got to his feet. "She served her purpose," he said, brushing off his tunic and leather armor. He had intended on keeping Astrid alive until she enchanted the tomb door with a camouflage spell. She'd already set magical barriers and booby traps throughout the underground structure in case anyone was foolish enough to come searching for the runestone. After that, he planned on killing her. The markers to the Eye of Odin had to remain a secret, that much was clear. Halfdan couldn't risk anyone knowing their location. Not a witch. Not a Varangian. Not anyone.

Not even a friend.

He drew a dagger from his belt and, before Solveig knew what was happening, drove the blade deep into his friend's stomach. He stabbed once, twice—the third thrust went to the hilt.

Solveig inhaled sharply. His hands fumbled, trying to wrap around Halfdan's throat.

"Forgive me, old friend," Halfdan whispered, lowering Solveig gently to the ground. The chokehold weakened. "You knew it had to end this way."

Solveig coughed. Blood bubbled from his mouth. "Curse you," he rasped. His face contorted in agony. "Curse you to the pits of Helheim."

Halfdan pulled the dagger from Solveig's gut and cleaned it on his sleeve. Treachery had become as much a part of his arsenal as his sword—often more useful. He knelt in front of his friend until the Viking drew his final breath.

There was no such thing as trust and friendship when it came to the Eye. Its power was too seductive, too tempting. Solveig was his friend, but he was also greedy and conniving. Not a good combination when stashing away and keeping secret a treasure that had the potential of destroying the world.

Still, unfortunate that he had to die—that they all did. He focused on the stone door. Another magicker would have to be commissioned to create a key and seal it. *That magicker would have to be disposed of as well*, Halfdan figured.

He returned the blade to its scabbard, and went about relieving Solveig of his valuables before rolling him to the ledge. With one final push, his friend's body plummeted, splashing into the seawater below.

"Let the sea guide your way to Valhalla."

Halfdan turned and climbed the stone stairway leading away from the tomb door. Solveig's last words replayed in his mind: "Curse you to the pits of Helheim."

Halfdan knew his journey to the afterlife would come soon enough. But there were still two markers to hide before then. After he completed his tasks, only the unlikely partnership of cunning and magic would be able to retrieve the runestones.

He had made sure of it.

And considering the traps, secret clues, and, in this case, a giant serpent, Halfdan wondered who'd be stupid enough to try.

Chapter 1

Present day
Istanbul, Turkey

The Viking longship *Drakkar* cut through the choppy waters of the Sea of Marmara, heading for a city that stretched across the full length of the horizon. Grayle Rowen hand-shaded his eyes, scanning the inlet dividing Istanbul's cosmopolitan center from the old, historic peninsula. Mosques, minarets and medieval fortifications were dotted between modern apartment blocks and sprawling gardens.

A far better sight than where he had come from.

Just this morning, Grayle had been in a fight for his life against Frost Giants and Hel, the goddess of death. They barely managed to escape with the information obtained from an evil Hex. That information led them here—to Istanbul—the possible location of another runestone marker leading to the Eye of Odin.

It had taken three hours to sail from the frozen reaches of Norway to the Turkish capital. Grayle had kept to himself through most of the voyage. He used the time to process what Sarah Finn

7

had revealed shortly after plucking him from Baldersted's freezing waters.

"You're a Hexhunter," she had said, someone who carried out assassinations and murdered witches centuries ago. Like him, Hexhunters were impervious to magic, were drawn to magical artifacts and did not possess an aura—the luminous energy surrounding living things.

"Am I dead?" Grayle had asked, too freaked out to understand everything she was telling him.

Sarah had laughed and assured him he was very much alive.

In turn, Grayle told her about his strange nightmares, the ones taking him back five years ago to his first memory, being found abandoned in Vancouver's Stanley Park in the dead of winter. He was only ten.

But despite their new honesty policy, Grayle still felt compelled to withhold bits of information from her, like his run-in with Odin or his personal reasons for wanting the Eye of Odin. Whether by choice or experience, he wasn't used to divulging information so freely, especially if he wasn't going to get something in return.

He glanced to where Sarah leaned on the opposite bow rail. She'd changed into a T-shirt and black cargo pants. She made the casual outfit look stylish. Her glossy black hair, tied into a ponytail, swayed in the crisp sea breeze. A pretty girl, one of the prettiest Grayle had ever seen. He'd never admit it though—especially not to her.

As if aware of his attention, Sarah walked over and settled next to him.

"Why are we slowing down?" Grayle asked, noticing the *Drakkar's* sail going slack.

"It's the buoys." Sarah gestured to the passing red beacons bobbing in the water. "They control the magic used by Folklorian vessels as they enter the harbor. It doesn't affect our camouflage, but it keeps us from speeding. Safety precautions."

Grayle nodded as if magical buoys were an everyday occurrence. "You really sure this is where we're supposed to go?" he asked as more of the city's historic skyline came into view.

Sarah brushed flyaways from her face. "Almost a hundred percent sure."

The question didn't escape her Caretaker's super hearing.

"Yer takin' an awful gamble," Grigsby shouted from the ship's rudder. "You realize what might happen if yer wrong?"

"I dinna think I am," Sarah hollered back. Her Scottish accent came out more when she argued with the elf. "The Hex mentioned the stone lies in *the capital of the east*. Istanbul was once Constantinople—a Roman city—the capital of the Eastern Roman Empire—"

"I know that. I was around when it *became* Istanbul," Grigsby replied.

Super hearing was only the beginning of the elf's quirkiness. Being 800 years old, he continuously reinvented his persona every century or so. Currently he fancied himself as a cowboy, like John Wayne. Hence the cowboy slang.

Grayle found it annoying. He wasn't a fan of the Caretaker, mostly because Grigsby wasn't a fan of him.

The Caretaker hefted his silver Winchester under one arm, then brought the rifle up to his shoulder and peered down its barrel. He grimaced. "*The capital of the east* can be any number of cities in these parts—Cairo…Damascus. Heck, it can even be Kiev or Baghdad. Halfdan traveled to all of 'em." He spit on the rifle and polished it with the sleeve of his duster.

"He also traveled to Constantinople," Sarah said, throwing him an impatient look. "After the Roman Empire fell, the remaining eastern provinces formed the Byzantine Empire and Constantinople became a rich, powerful city. But like any empire, it eventually lost its wealth and prestige. Several invaders, including the Vikings, plundered the city. The emperor of Byzantium was so impressed with the Vikings, he actually asked them to stay and act as his personal bodyguard. They became known as Varangians."

"Varangians. That's what Brenna overheard the Hex saying." Grayle recalled the blonde witch's rushed explanation before escaping into the bifrost.

"Exactly. But I think the Varangians guarded more than just the emperor. I think they were left behind to safeguard one of the runestones."

"I hope yer right," Grigsby said, leaning on the rudder. "'Cause if not, we just came a long way for nothin'."

The *Drakkar* steered left into the Golden Horn estuary and nosed into one of the city's ancient harbors. Five wooden ships lay anchored in the bay. Each was over a hundred feet long. Like the *Drakkar*, a single sail was hoisted on the center mast of each ship. The horrible face of Medusa was stitched into the fabric of all five ships. Spinnakers also bulged from the ships' bows and holes dotted the sides where oar blades stuck out. Grayle counted at least thirty on one side. Large eyes were painted on the forward hulls above long battering rams that jutted from the ships just above the water line. they looked like the horns of some water-bound rhinoceros. Compared to the modern vessels around them, the wooden ships seemed out-of-place.

"Aren't those Greek triremes?" Grayle asked, recognizing them from his history books.

Sarah shook her head. "They're Roman." She pointed to the trireme's aft section. "Greek ships never had those." A giant crossbow called a ballista sat mounted on a swiveling platform; the weapon could shoot six-foot arrows from any angle.

A man stood next to the nearest trireme's mainsail, eying them suspiciously. He wore a finely sculpted breastplate cast to look like muscles. Below his metal torso, straps of brown leather hung over a red tunic. His knees were bare despite the crisp air, and he clasped a bronze helmet under one arm.

"We've been spotted," Sarah called out.

Grigsby nodded, his expression turned grimmer than usual—if that was even possible. The Caretaker usually had a bad case of perma-frown.

"Aren't we disguised as a yacht or something?" Grayle asked.

"A fishing trolley—but that's how we appear to Outlanders. Folklorians can see through our camouflage spells."

The *Drakkar* glided by the triremes without incident and eased into a marina packed with pleasure crafts, water taxis, and fishermen selling their day's catch straight from their boats. The longship nudged along an empty dock. Sarah vaulted the port rail and tied off the bowline, while Grayle tightened the stern ropes to a T-shaped metal cleat.

The metallic clink of Grigsby's spurs jingled as he trudged across a plank pushed onto the pier. "We gotta get a wiggle on," he said. "If the Romans reported our arrival, we won't have much time to do whatever we gotta do." He fit his Stetson cowboy hat over his pointed ears. "I take it you got a plan?"

Sarah was already tramping up the dock. "I do. Follow me."

Chapter 2

From his lofty view seated in one of Istanbul's swankier cafés, Sebastian Caine could scan every yacht and sailboat entering the Golden Horn. The estuary bustled with traffic. Giant tankers and cargo freighters criss-crossed the open water, leaving just enough space for ferries and other smaller vessels to navigate between them.

The billionaire sipped his coffee. It tasted bitter, matching his mood.

Twice now, his bodyguard had failed to capture this Grayle Rowen. Mussels reported how he lost the boy during the Frost Giant attack, catching a glimpse of him diving into the frigid fjord waters before being whisked away by a waiting ship.

Mussels can't be held entirely responsible for his failure.

Caine glanced at the blonde woman seated next to him. Even now, Hel's darkness radiated from her shifted form. She wore Chanel sunglasses, immaculate makeup, red lipstick, and hair coiffed in a classic bob cut. She would have been attractive had Caine not known the true horror that lurked underneath.

Inwardly, he hated relying on the goddess of death. For the moment, however, Hel had her uses. She had correctly predicted the Hexhunter's journey to the Hex and had also managed to sneak her way into Midgard, a feat he still hadn't been able to solve. Beings from the other Nine Norse Realms, especially the Underworlds, were prohibited from entering Folklore strongholds.

So how did she do it?

The goddess had also struck a deal with the Frost Giants in order to secure the Hexhunter's capture. She failed to mention she needed to kidnap a girl as an offering to the Hex though. Caine wasn't opposed to ridding the world of another witch, but he found cannibalism most distasteful. Yet, for all her powers and connections, the teenagers had escaped.

They could be anywhere by now.

Caine took a deep, cleansing breath.

No, the Hex told Mussels about Varangians and the capital of the East. They'll be coming here. But their vessel would take longer...to...get...to..."

He set his coffee cup down with a loud *clink*.

A fishing trolley gliding into the harbor caught his eye. It looked unremarkable—white, forty feet long, with just enough wear and tear to blend in with the surrounding traffic. It drifted over the water, maneuvering past ferryboats and cargo ships, winking in and out between giant cruise ships moored along the waterfront. Caine couldn't be sure this was the vessel he'd been waiting for—maybe years of witch hunting and chasing magical artifacts had given him a sixth sense—but when the vessel docked in the marina below, his instincts were proven correct. The witch and Hexhunter emerged, followed closely by a tall man donning a cowboy hat and trench coat.

The witch's Caretaker, Caine presumed.

He turned his attention to the boy, studying his features. No photographs existed of Grayle Rowen. Looking at him from a distance, Caine couldn't help being unimpressed. Somehow, he'd thought a Hexhunter would stand out more, his physical presence matching his true importance. He saw nothing more than a teenager with messy hair and a slight, athletic build.

"Look sharp," Caine alerted the goddess.

Hel looked up from her Vogue magazine. She slid her Chanel sunglasses down her nose and followed Caine's gaze.

Sarah Finn led the boy and Caretaker toward the marina's exit. Their route was hurried and purposeful, quickly crossing the Kennedy Caddesi and heading into the heart of the old city.

"They know where to go next," Caine said. "We'll wait and see where they lead us. If they've tracked down another stone, we can take it from them. I will contact the others. I need you to—"

Hel vanished in a burst of smoke and brimstone before he could finish. The magazine she'd been reading dropped on the table. No one in the café seemed to notice.

Caine cursed under his breath. Given the chance, he knew Hel would take the remaining runestone for herself. How much could he trust her? How long could their partnership last? *She could ruin everything.* He got up quickly, placed a handful of Turkish liras on the table, and exited the café.

Pedestrians crammed the main avenue, but tailing the teenagers presented little difficulty. The Caretaker's bobbing cowboy hat could be spotted from a block away. Their trajectory pointed straight to an enormous structure resting on a hilltop.

Caine took out his cell phone and dialed.

Mussels answered. "Oui, chef?"

"I know where they're going. Meet me outside the Hagia Sophia's south entrance in ten minutes. Have the others on standby."

"D'accord."

Caine paused. "No mistakes this time," he added sternly, "or we might have to discuss your severance package."

Mussels understood the implied threat. "Oui, chef."

Caine pocketed the phone. He had access to two runestone fragments already. Soon he would have a third. It was only a matter of time before all five were in his possession.

Providing Hel doesn't double-cross me before then.

He closed his eyes, envisioning the moment he held the Eye of Odin in his hands. Years of planning would finally come to fruition. Millions would die—the price of global change. But despite the horror, Caine's lips curled slightly at the corners.

It will be a new world, a safer world—free of witches, warlocks, gods and goddesses.

And I will be its architect.

Chapter 3

Istanbul's traffic was chaotic. Scooters, run-down beaters, motorcycles, and freight trucks honked and screeched their way down a wide street with little regard for road signs or lane markers.

Grayle, Sarah, and Grigsby waited several minutes before a break in traffic allowed them to cross safely into the city's pedestrian zone. Once there, they weaved through a cultural melting pot of ethnicities, the young and old, families and businessmen, all going about their daily lives. Tourists strolled the wide pavements and filled the outdoor tables of fancy restaurants that overlooked the crowded marina. Enticing smells from cafés blended into a sweet aroma of exotic spices and espresso coffee.

A huge dome climbed twenty stories above the rooftops ahead. Its polished copper surface glowed purple in the afternoon sun.

"Look." Grayle pointed to where a golden crescent moon topped the building's arched roof. "*Under crescent moon it rests in sleep,* that's what the runestone inscriptions said."

Sarah nodded. "I know. That's where we're going."

Before Hel had stolen the runestone marker from the Vancouver Museum, Sarah had the good sense to snap photos of its inscriptions. Grayle remembered the first two lines:

> *The All-Father's eye waits in caverns deep,*
> *Under crescent moon it rests in sleep.*

There was another line mentioning destiny favoring the bold and something about Ragnarok, the Viking version of the apocalypse. Preventing the catastrophe was why they were trying to find the Eye of Odin in the first place.

Well, Sarah and Grigsby's reason anyway.

Grayle had other motives. If what he heard about the Eye was true, that whoever possessed it had the power to see into the past, present, and future, he could use it to find out where he came from, who his parents were. But Grayle doubted Sarah, the elf, or the Vikings would let him near it.

I'll have to find a way.

"You think the next clue to finding the Eye is in there?" he asked.

"The Hagia Sophia is the only building still standing that existed during the Viking Age. It's the best place to start."

They climbed a series of steps leading to a lengthy, tree-lined walkway. Water fountains spewed in rhythmic patterns to their left, while merchants sold carpets, tobacco and Turkish souvenirs to the right.

Grayle swiped a brochure from a nearby display. He unfolded it and read aloud: "The Hagia Sophia was first built in 537 CE. Once a church, later a mosque and now a museum, it was the world's largest cathedral for almost a thousand years. In the past, the church contained a large collection of holy relics, many of them taken when Constantinople was attacked by Crusaders in 1206…"

"Crusaders who happened to be soldiers for the Inquisition," Sarah pointed out.

Grigsby spat on the pavement. "Freakin' Crossers—bin responsible for so much death an' mayhem."

"Crossers is what Folklorians call them," Sarah explained. "Anything in there about runestones?"

Grayle skimmed the pamphlet and shook his head.

They reached a plaza facing the old church.

At first glance, the Hagia Sophia was a combination of bulging domes and buttresses. Countless arched windows dotted the outer walls, walls that changed from a smooth plaster to roughly exposed brick. Even the colors appeared mismatched. As if brushed by a preschooler, parts of the Hagia were painted terracotta or left in their original dark gray and marble white. Yet despite its misshapen architecture and awkward color scheme, next to Midgard's Great Hall, it was the most impressive building Grayle had ever seen.

"Let's say this is the right place," Grigsby said. "How're you gonna gain entry into that gospel mill without raisin' suspicion? You got no money an' sneakin' in can only lead you into a heap o' trouble."

Sarah's face went blank. Grayle could tell she hadn't thought that far ahead.

"I can start a fuss an' skedaddle in time," Grigsby offered, "givin' you two a chance to get in." He padded the Winchester beneath his trench coat.

"The last thing we need is a shoot-out and ending up on the six o'clock news," Grayle muttered.

"I don't hear you comin' up with anythin' better, kid."

Grayle scanned the colossal building. A spike-topped iron fence ran around the complex. The bars were too closely spaced to squeeze through. There was no way to get inside—none that he could see, anyway.

Maybe there's an emergency exit or an unattended delivery door?

His gaze fixed on eight tour buses parked along the plaza. A steady stream of tourists gathered shoulder to shoulder outside the main entrance.

"We could always take a tour," he said.

Sarah lifted an eyebrow. "Another tour?"

Grayle understood her hesitation. There were things he'd rather subject himself to: detention, an algebra test, a root canal. Not to mention the fact their last museum tour nearly got them killed. Their options, however, were limited.

"It's almost 3:30. The museum closes—" he consulted the brochure, "— in an hour. Enough time to get inside and have a look around."

"But you got no dineros," Grigsby said. "How're you gonna pay?"

"Look at the tour buses, the fancy cameras, the awful Cabana shirts," Grayle pointed out. "Those tourists must be from one of the cruise ships in the harbor."

"So?"

"So…cruise ship excursions are prepaid. All passengers need to do is get on the right bus and they're driven to their chosen attraction. No money exchanged, no money required. If we pretend to be part of a group, there's a good chance we'll get in for free and unnoticed."

"What happens if you don't?" the Caretaker challenged.

Grayle grew tired of butting heads with the elf. "Then I'll improvise!" he said bluntly and trudged toward the Hagia Sophia.

Chapter 4

"**H**is plan's worth a shot," Sarah said, watching Grayle march away.

She was worried about him. He'd shown remarkable resilience in the past two days: being attacked by a goddess of death, learning about Folklore, the existence of witches, and—not three hours ago—that he could be a Hexhunter, a particularly rare and dangerous enemy of Folklore. She couldn't help feeling the boy she pulled from Baldersted's icy fjord was different from the one who had saved her from Hel inside the Vancouver Museum. There was an even deeper coldness about him now, as tangible as the freezing waters she plucked him from.

Grigsby grabbed her arm. "When are you gonna wise up to the sorta trouble that boy'll get you in...*has* gotten you in?"

"I told you, I know what I'm doing." The words sounded weak, even to her. "We still don't know for sure what Grayle is yet. He shows all the signs of being a Hexhunter, but what about his other abilities? Not being able to be seen by cameras? Runes glowing when he's near? You know *those* don't belong to a Hexhunter."

"All of a sudden yer an expert on Hexhunters?" Grigsby let go of her arm and gently placed both palms on her shoulder. "I'm just lookin' out for you. You know that, right?"

She nodded. "I do, but I have to do this…for Mum's sake."

His hard green eyes stared into hers. Sarah wondered how many times he'd looked at her mother the same way. Grigs had been her Caretaker too.

Before she was killed by that butcher of a billionaire.

The elf pulled her close and folded his arms around her. "I can't lose the both of you," he said.

Sarah buried her face in his duster. The rawhide smelled musky. "You won't."

Grigs cleared his throat and slowly pushed her away. "Alright, alright. Go on—before I get all sentimental-like." He leaned against a lamppost and tipped his hat low. "I reckon I'll stand guard out here. I can feel the gospel mill's pelma from here."

The pelma was a magical barrier preventing elves and other Mythic Races from entering certain Folklore strongholds. At first the barriers were meant to prevent attacks from the more warlike races, like centaurs and ogres. Eventually, the pelma extended to all races considered undesirable, which included pretty much all of them.

"It's not fair," Sarah said. Restricting others from entering places based on race was wrong.

Grigs shrugged, downplaying his frustration. "It is what it is. No use griping about it." He spat on the pavement. "Make sure you got everythin' you need before you go."

Sarah opened her laptop bag, checking the contents inside: One minimized, life-saving, magical shield. *Check.* A new, waterproof cell phone. *Check.* One new laptop upgraded with Folklore's most recent software. *Check.*

"It's all here," she said, closing the pink flap. "We'll come out as soon as we find something. If we even get in."

She hurried across the plaza, catching up to Grayle as he slipped into a queue of gray-haired tourists. They parked behind a woman wearing a wide-brimmed hat.

"Mr. Sunshine not coming with us?" he asked, glancing over her shoulder.

Sarah shook her head. "He'll wait for us out here. Are you sure this is going to work?" she asked, scanning the colossal church's exterior.

Grayle flashed a self-assured grin. "I'm an expert at getting into places, remember?"

"Yeah, your break-ins are good, but your break-*outs* need work…*remember*? I don't want to be dragging your sorry butt out of *this* museum too."

"Don't worry. That's not gonna happen."

"Right. Famous last words."

A girl wearing a traditional Muslim headscarf appeared in front of their group. She was young, maybe seventeen or eighteen, with coppery skin and brown eyes shaped like almonds.

"Good afternoon," she said, speaking with a British accent. "My name is Nazan, and I will be your guide."

Sarah dropped her mental shield and focused on the girl's aura. As an Auralex, she was able to see the life essences of living things. They appeared as a luminescent glow surrounding a person's body.

She flinched.

The "gift" of aura-seeing came with a heavy price. Not only did Auralexes see auras, they also felt the emotions of anyone within a hundred yards. Sarah had to learn to tune out the emotional assault that caused most Auralexes pain and, if exposed for too long, to go insane. Letting her guard drop now, the rushing waves of excitement, worry, sadness, joy, and heartache bombarded her.

She quickly scanned the tourists in her vicinity. Only the tour guide's aura shimmered red.

She was Folklorian.

But from which Folklore? Roman? Byzantine? Ottoman? Persian?

Sensing auras had its limits. Sarah could tell the difference between an Outlander and Folklorian. She could even read the fluctuations in a person's aura to tell whether they were happy, angry, or being deceitful. But she couldn't tell which particular Folklore a person came from.

Nazan opened the gates and waved the tour group inside. She spotted Sarah and Grayle at the back. "I'm pleased to see we have some younger visitors."

Sarah kept her face downcast, but Grayle nudged closer to an elderly couple wearing oversized sunglasses, the kind that made seniors look like wrinkled insects.

"Grandma and grandpa made us come," he moped.

The elderly couple looked at one another, confused, but said nothing as the group made their way in.

Sarah eyeballed Grayle. He grinned and brushed by her.

Chapter 5

Brenna Bjorndottir hurried through the Great Hall's darkened corridors.

Late—as usual.

Loremaster Onem had called a mission debriefing a half hour ago. An explanation was needed for what happened in Baldersted this morning. Brenna would have reported in sooner, had the return journey from the northern city not taken three hours. Prince Lothar couldn't seem to get the bifrost incantation right. Could it have been his frayed nerves after confronting the Hex and Frost Giants? Or was it the blood spewing from his broken nose, courtesy of Sarah Finn's fist? Either way, it took him four more attempts to channel the magical bridge to its proper destination.

Brenna played nervously with the ends of her white-blonde hair, tied into a single long braid over her shoulder. Before being summoned, she had just enough time to soak in a warm bath and change from her filthy nightgown into her warrior dress. Made from stiff leather, animal hides, and bits of hand-beaten metal, the outfit had belonged to her mother when she was fourteen. The only difference was an underlayer of dragonhide sewn around the waist like a protective corset.

I'm never going to take this off again, Brenna vowed.

Being kidnapped had been bad enough—kidnapped in nothing more than a flimsy nightgown was downright embarrassing. The only visible evidence of her ordeal was an ugly purple bruise along her hairline. But no matter how much she bathed or switched her wardrobe, the memories of her abduction would be harder to wash away.

Her father, Bjorn Ragnarson, walked beside her. He hadn't said much since she got back. It was difficult for him to believe the girl he shared breakfast with this morning, kissed on the forehead, and said good luck to was actually Hel, the goddess of death, shapeshifted into Brenna's form. He didn't realize his daughter had been kidnapped in the middle of the night, used as payment to get information from a Hex. The payment being Brenna's life—her flesh—stored in a trunk like some plucked chicken.

"Do not offer the Loremaster any additional information than what he asks," her father said.

Brenna's fingers traced the magic coin in her pocket. Sarah had given it to her before escaping Baldersted.

Find your father, Sarah had said. *Tell him everything that's happened, no one else. Not even Loremaster Onem.*

"Not even Loremaster Onem," Brenna whispered.

"What?" her father asked.

She cleared her throat. "Do you suspect Onem of something?"

The banded tattoo stretching across her father's face crinkled. "The old man uses information to meet his own selfish needs. I don't want you to offer anything that might be turned against you."

"That shouldn't be problem," Brenna said. "I was locked in a crate for most of the ordeal. There isn't much I can offer."

"All the same…watch what you say around him."

She nodded, then switched her attention to the boy trailing three paces behind them. "What's Svein doing here?"

"He is here for protection."

"Protection? For who…me? I don't need some dungas to protect me."

Svein didn't react to being called a *dungas*—Norse for 'useless person'. Focused on his cell phone, he was oblivious to anything going on around him.

He was sixteen, already known as a skilled fighter, and handsome, even though Brenna tried to ignore that part. She, like most magickers, had no time for relationships. Still, it was hard not to notice the blond hair hanging past his shoulders, his well-proportioned muscles, and a jawline that made the other girls swoon.

"Whoever allowed Hel into the city to kidnap you will know the real you is back," Bjorn argued. "He may want to silence you for good, if only to keep his identity a secret."

"Or *her* identity." Three-quarters of magically-talented Folklorians were women after all.

"So you either accept Svein's protection, or I ship you off to your mother in Danemark."

Brenna pressed her lips together to keep from using every curse word she knew. She hated ultimatums but couldn't blame her father for being overprotective. If a traitor was out there, the last thing Bjorn Ragnarson wanted was to see his daughter in danger.

"I am *not* leaving," Brenna said firmly. She had a job to do—flush out the traitor who allowed Hel to snatch her from her own bed.

"Very well," Bjorn grumbled. "Honestly, I should never have let you join the Hex mission in the first place."

"I don't need *your* permission when it comes to magicker business," Brenna shot back. "I'm old enough to make my own decisions."

"I seriously doubt that."

Brenna felt the heat rise in her face. She was about to say something snarky when they arrived at the Loremaster's laboratory.

"Keep watch out here," Bjorn told Svein.

The boy looked up from his phone briefly and nodded, then sat on a bench around the corner.

At least he does as he's told, Brenna thought.

Her father turned to leave.

"You're not coming in?" Brenna asked. She didn't want to go in alone.

"I wasn't invited. And I have other matters to attend to." He must have noticed Brenna's apprehension. "You'll be fine," he added. "You are an heir of House Lodbrok after all. Don't forget that. And remember not to give up information freely…*and* keep your emotions in check."

"What's that supposed to mean?"

"You know exactly what it means. You have the same temper as your mother."

"I don't have—" Brenna stopped, realizing she was yelling. "I don't have a temper," she finished more calmly.

Her father smirked. His smugness was annoying.

"Fine. Do what you need to do," she said. "I got this."

With that, Brenna turned on her heel and marched into the laboratory.

Chapter 6

Ten minutes into the museum tour and Sarah was ready to bolt. Their group moved agonizingly slow. It started with a leisurely walk across the Hagia Sophia's outer complex. Towering minarets dominated its four corners like stone rockets, having once called faithful Muslims to prayer. The tourists stopped and gathered close while Nazan spun tales of famous Sultans, brutal murders, and unsolved mysteries. Any other time, Sarah would have found the stories fascinating, but this wasn't a sightseeing tour—not for her and Grayle anyway.

They finally arrived at a set of ancient bronze doors leading into the museum's atrium. Marble slabs covered the walls and floor. Mosaics adorned the ceiling.

"Since the museum had once been a mosque, according to Islamic customs, pictures were not allowed," Nazan explained. "Therefore, the Ottomans, who conquered Constantinople in the fifteenth century, did away with the Christian look of the church. They covered most of the original frescoes and mosaics with Islamic designs. But as you can see above us..." She gestured to an arch over the doorway, where pieces of colored stone were carefully arranged to create three rigid figures. "Our restoration teams have uncovered many of the church's original mosaics. This one, of Emperor Justinian, Mary, and baby Jesus, originated in the Middle Ages, a thousand years after the Hagia Sophia was built."

From the corner of her eye, Sarah saw Grayle's hand shoot up.

"What are you doing?" she whispered.

"What does it look like? I'm asking a question."

"Be careful," she warned, scrutinizing the white-haired travelers surrounding them. "We're in the Roman Folklore now. If anyone suspects anything, we could have Roman agents breathing down our necks. For all we know, one of these geriatrics could be one of them."

"What are they going to do…beat me with their walkers? Don't worry. I'll be discreet."

The guide noticed Grayle's hand. "Yes?"

"Is it true that Vikings attacked Constantinople centuries ago?"

Sarah rolled her eyes. *Does he even know the meaning of discreet?*

"Yes. In fact, the Vikings attacked the city on three separate occasions."

"Did they leave anything behind?"

"You mean besides a path of death and destruction?" Nazan quipped, bringing chuckles from the rest of the group.

"No, I mean did they leave any artifacts?"

The guide thought for a moment. "Our restoration teams are uncovering new relics every week. But I'm afraid nothing of Viking origin. However, there are some Viking runes in different parts of the museum."

"Where?"

"On the top floor of the southern gallery, but we don't have time to see them." Nazan's voice hinted at impatience. "Now if you'll follow me," she re-addressed the rest of the group, "we'll

continue into the Hagia Sophia's east wing. Here we can find…"
Her voice trailed off as the tour shuffled on without them.

Sarah turned to Grayle. "Runes," she said, unable to hide her
excitement.

Together, they dashed up a polished staircase to the second
level.

It wasn't hard to guess where the runes were located. A different
group of elderly tourists huddled along a marble parapet, a low
protective wall overlooking the Hagia Sophia's central nave.

Sarah pushed, ducked, and squeezed through the crowd. She
peered over a woman's shoulder. Scrawled on the parapet's surface
were three runes, nothing more than incoherent letters scratched
onto the surface.

"That's it?" Grayle blurted out behind her.

Sarah glared at him, mouthing the words *Roman agents*. She
went over and whispered in his ear, "We can't investigate with all
these people around."

He must have taken it as a sign to do something, because the
next thing she knew he snatched the cell phone from her bag and
held it to his ear without dialling.

"Hi Mom," he said, raising his voice so everyone could hear.
"It's great to hear from you. What? You're going to have to speak
up, I can't hear you!"

The seniors around him scowled. Another rude teenager spoil-
ing their day.

Immune to their stares, Grayle continued his imaginary conversation. "You heard back from the doctor? He said what? I'm highly
contagious?"

Sarah watched as annoyed looks evaporated into concern.

"The virus is airborne? I shouldn't be around nursing mothers,
children or the *elderly*?"

At that point, Grayle let out a wracking cough so long and hoarse Sarah thought he ruptured a lung.

Like magic, the seniors around him took several steps back.

Grayle coughed again, this time turning into full convulsions, sending the tour group hobbling for the stairs.

"Piece of cake," Grayle said once the last senior disappeared. He handed back her phone.

Sarah shook her head and set about examining the runes. She read the English caption fastened next to the runic scribbles, wrong spelling and all:

> "*The Viking's graffitties are illegible except for the name…Halvdan…It dates 9th century.*"

Her brow furrowed. "So Halfdan was definitely here. But something about these letters doesn't make sense. Wait a second…" She took Grayle's hand in hers and placed it on the parapet. She felt a tingling excitement as more runes slowly shimmered into view, glowing brighter and filling in the incomplete letters.

"What does it say?" Grayle asked, careful to keep his connection with the marble's smooth surface.

Sarah did her best to translate:

> "*Follow straight to columns forth,*
> *Finding there your points of worth.*

Seek thou runes to guide your way,
And find at peril the serpent's doorway."

"Serpent's doorway. Ring any bells?" Grayle asked.

Sarah's mind drew a blank. "No idea. But according to this, we have to find more runes."

"Where do we start?"

"*Follow straight to columns forth*. We start looking at columns, I guess."

"But which ones? We're not going to have time to search them all."

He was right. From where they stood, Sarah saw over fifty pillars of various shapes and sizes, spread throughout the Hagia Sophia's interior on different levels. It would take hours to examine them all.

There had to be something they overlooked.

Sarah examined the glowing inscriptions again, searching for some sign that would help them. "Look at this letter." She pointed to a rune resembling an arrow.

↑

"This is the symbol of Tyr, the Norse god of war. It has the same sound as our letter T."

"So? There's a few of them."

"But out of all the letters, they're slightly off-center…each one of them. See? That was done on purpose." Sarah smiled. "I think they're aiming toward the first rune."

She followed the direction in which the "arrows" pointed, gazing across the main dome where a row of ebony columns supported a smaller half-dome.

She pointed. "Those ones."

Grayle removed his hand. The runes faded from sight. "Let's go," he said.

They flew down the marble stairs, almost knocking into several Japanese tourists.

"Yavaslatmak!" a Turkish security guard shouted—*slow down*—or what Sarah thought meant slow down. Her Turkish was rusty.

Reaching the main level, they slowed to a jog and arrived at the opposite set of pillars.

They got to work, inspecting each column—eight in all. If there was a rune written on them somewhere, centuries of wear and tear made it difficult to distinguish it from a crack or scuff mark.

Before long, Sarah found faint scratches too straight to have occurred by accident and easily overlooked, especially if one didn't know what to look for.

"Psst…over here," she whispered.

Grayle rushed to her side. "It's another arrow—"

"Pointing across the church again," Sarah finished.

Scanning the direction in which the new arrow pointed, they had ten pillars to search: four large columns of black and gray marble and six smaller ebony columns in the galleria above.

"Maybe we should split up," Grayle suggested, wiping his hands on his pants. "We'll cover more ground that way."

"No. I may need your touch to reveal the rune."

They raced to the other side, drawing frowns as they cut off more tourists.

Spotting the next rune proved harder. These pillars were taller by another four feet, and the lighter marble hid the wear better than those made of ebony. Chunks of the pillars' bases were also missing, hacked off or battered over the centuries. But as Sarah's eyes grew accustomed to the marble's shaded patterns, she found the rune on the fourth column. It was faint, no more than a shadow worn into the surface of the limestone.

"Found it," she said, running her fingers over the mark. Another T rune, this time angling slightly to the left. "It's pointing over there."

They crossed the museum a third time and found the rune almost right away. But no arrow directed them where to go this time; it was just a single letter etched prominently in the center column.

X

"I don't understand. What symbol is that?" Grayle asked.

Sarah frowned. "It's called gebo. It's like our letter G."

"What does it stand for? Gee, I fooled you? Gee, you're a bunch of idiots?"

"Calm down," Sarah said. "The mark is obviously trying to tell us something. If there aren't any more arrow runes telling us where to go, we need to believe this is the last one. Since it's different from all the rest, it must have some special significance."

"Well, it just looks like an X to me," Grayle grumbled.

"There is no letter for X in the futhark alphabet." Then it dawned on her. "Unless…Do you still have that brochure?"

He took it out of his back pocket and handed it to her.

Sarah flattened the paper on the marble floor. "What if the gebo rune isn't supposed to be a letter? What if it *is* an X?"

She examined a sketch of the Hagia Sophia's interior pictured on the brochure's outer flap. Grayle shifted to get a better look, hovering shoulder to shoulder with her.

"The Halfdan inscription was here." She pointed on the map. "If we draw a line from it to the second rune…" She traced the path with her finger. "And then a line from the third to the fourth, they intersect here." Her finger stopped at the center of the map. The lines converged under the Hagia Sophia's main dome. "X marks the spot."

"Or G marks the spot."

They allowed themselves a chuckle.

"I think we did it," Sarah whispered. "I think we found the runestone."

Chapter 7

The Loremaster's lab gave Brenna the creeps.

She'd been in this room not too long ago, being reprimanded after accidentally lighting the practice gymnasium on fire…a wayward flame spell gone wrong. Practical magic wasn't her area of expertise. Brenna was a Dyr'talara, a witch able to communicate with animals. She had no use for incineration spells, elixirs, or other kinds of sorcery.

She grimaced. *Or smelly lairs like this.*

The lab was a large, oval room. Jars, numbering in the thousands, filled curved shelves lining the walls and rising all the way to the ceiling. Skeletons and half-developed embryos, some twisted and malformed, floated in cloudy jars of various sizes. Labels written in runes described the contents inside. A collection of the weird and dangerous of Folklore.

The heavy door groaned as Brenna closed it.

Haakon spotted her first. He rushed over. His black, braided beard swished from side to side on his round belly. Tattoos of tangled Norse designs covered his arms. Even without his trademark bearskin draped over his shoulders, Midgard's Jarl was an imposing figure. "Where have you been?" he asked, visibly annoyed.

"Washing up and getting changed," she said.

Haakon had a strange odor about him—something acrid, sour and metallic. Brenna wasn't sure if the smell came from him or the awful smells abundant in the room.

He took her by the elbow and led her to where Loremaster Onem, Erik the Red, and Lothar huddled around a table placed in the center of the room.

The wrinkles on Onem's shaven scalp deepened when he saw her. His withered body stood crooked, weighed down by his age and a heavy green embroidered cloak. "Now that we're all here, we can finally begin," he grumbled.

Brenna didn't apologize. If the old man had been through what she'd experienced, he would have allowed himself a bath and a change of clothes too. She was about to tell him so when she noticed a tall woman standing among them.

Brenna's jaw dropped, recognizing the red flowing robes of a Wicca.

A representative from the Supreme Coven…here?

Wiccas rarely made visits unless situations demanded their attention—like imminent threats to Folklore.

The woman looked like one of the models from an Outlander fashion magazine: tall and elegant, with straight red hair framing a flawless, milky white complexion. The folds of her red cloak hung from her slender frame in crisp, clean lines. And from her delicate neck hung a ruby amulet the likes Brenna had never seen before. But Brenna wasn't fooled by her elegance and beauty. The Wicca radiated power. Brenna suspected that if they shook hands, she'd feel a jolt of energy.

Onem cleared his throat. "We are pleased to have Wicca Malin join us in order to ascertain what happened—"

"We can dispense with the formalities and get right to it," the Wicca interrupted.

The Loremaster's cataract eye twitched, clearly annoyed at being cut off.

"Let's begin with the troubling news that may jeopardize the very existence of Folklore," Malin said, addressing the group. "Loremasters around the world are being notified as we speak, but, for the time being, I must ask that what I am about to reveal remain confined to this room."

Everyone nodded except for Erik, who kept his usual frozen scowl.

"The boy accompanying the magickers to Baldersted this morning was a Hexhunter."

The Wicca stayed quiet for a moment, letting the information sink in.

Brenna's heart pounded. She remembered Lothar saying something shortly before Sarah kicked him into the bifrost: *He's a Hexhunter, Sarah. Do you think my father or anyone else will let him live beyond his usefulness?*

"That can't be," Brenna said. "The last Hexhunters were exterminated centuries ago."

Haakon huffed. "Apparently not."

"And you let him live?" growled Erik. He didn't seem surprised at the news. "You even let him go on a mission…with my son?" Lothar winced as Erik put a meaty hand on his shoulder.

The Jarl set his jaw. "At the time, using the boy and his skills seemed like a good idea. He does not know he is a Hexhunter, and is unaware of the true extent of his importance."

"What importance?" Brenna blurted out.

"As much as Hexhunters presented a danger to Folklore in the past," Onem explained, "they also displayed an uncanny ability to be drawn to magic—even more keenly than most Auralexes. Probably an inherent skill that made them such efficient hunters. We hoped to use the boy's abilities to find the next marker to the Eye of Odin."

"And that was poor judgment on your part," Malin said, "to be dealt with another time."

Onem and Haakon's gazes dropped to the floor.

"For now, the Coven is more concerned that Sarah Finn is involved in matters beyond her control. If she is indeed working with a Hexhunter, there may be unforeseeable consequences."

Brenna had known Sarah since their days at the Magicker Training Academy in Germany. They'd become fast friends, coming to one another's aid to take down a pompous bully. Since that day, Brenna knew Sarah was never the type to hold back or shy away from doing what was right. But this was different. She wasn't taking down some jerk warlock.

"You know Sarah wouldn't do anything to jeopardize Folklore's safety," Brenna said.

"No. I do not *know* that." The Wicca glared. "What I *do* know are the facts: Finn did not inform the Coven of the Hexhunter's existence. She has also disobeyed the Coven's orders in the past, taking it upon herself to make decisions that a young witch should not. She does not even possess the training or power to deal with a Hexhunter, let alone the Eye of Odin, a Level Five artifact."

Brenna couldn't argue there. Folklorian relics were levelled according to power and potential for world devastation. Most teen magickers were sent to retrieve Level Ones or Twos and, on rare occasions, Level Threes. Level Five artifacts could be Earth shattering—much too powerful for a novice witch to handle. Brenna knew that. So did Sarah.

"Why would she be going after the Eye on her own?" Brenna asked.

"I believe she is set on finding the artifact that indirectly led to her mother's death," said Onem. "Rachel Finn was killed while retrieving one of the runestone markers. Since then, Sarah has become infatuated with the Eye, and she now has a vital clue to the next marker's whereabouts."

"But so do we. What clue did the Hex provide you with in Baldersted?" Haakon directed toward Lothar.

The prince straightened, his usual smug attitude dialed down a notch. Normally, Lothar Erikson had no problem making everyone aware of how important he was. Right now, he actually looked pathetic. Sarah had broken his nose shortly before kicking him into the bifrost this morning, leaving the soft tissue under his eyes a deep purple. Sweat glistened beneath his short-cropped hair and his face had turned red, accentuating every freckle on his baby-fat cheeks.

He cleared his throat and recited what he'd learned from the Hex:

> *"Halfdan sought the All-Father's Eye,*
> *In caverns deep and mountains high,*
> *But in the capital of the east,*
> *The quest for glory he did cease."*

"The capital of the east?" Onem repeated.

"Did she mean Novgorod?" Erik grumbled. "Maybe Moscow?"

"It could be Istanbul or even further east," said Haakon.

"It may also be Baghdad," Onem added. "One runestone had been found there already. It would be a trick worthy of Loki to hide two runestones in the same city."

Haakon nodded. "And Baghdad is where Sarah's mother was killed. She may choose to go there for sentimental reasons."

Brenna didn't think so. What Lothar and the others couldn't know was the exchange she'd overheard between the Hex and the muscle-bound Outlander that had brought her to the dark witch's lair. Even though Brenna was locked in a trunk at the time, bits and pieces of conversation filtered through. She heard one word in particular: *Varangians*. It had meant something to Sarah, sparking some kind of understanding—a vital piece of the clue not mentioned by the Hex in her rhyme. One thing was for sure, Brenna wasn't about to offer up the extra intel.

"It may be wise to put a bounty on our renegade witch," Onem concluded.

Haakon slammed his fist on the table. "Why did Sarah not return to Midgard with the Hexhunter and the Hex's information when she had the chance? The mission was over."

"Because there is a traitor in Midgard, my lord," Brenna said, surprised the others hadn't clued in. "Someone let Hel into the city, through our defenses, so she could kidnap me."

The Loremaster gave her an incredulous look. "Why would the Death Queen go through all the trouble of entering our fortified city in order to kidnap a puny—" he paused, changing his choice of words—"a *young* witch as yourself? What would she have to gain?"

"To take my place. She knew I was going on the mission to Baldersted. Which means she knew of our plans *before* she entered the city. I think she wanted Grayle—the Hexhunter, I mean."

The last statement brought uncomfortable looks.

"Did she succeed?" Haakon asked. "Did she capture the boy?"

Lothar shook his head. "Sarah forced us to leave before we knew what became of them."

"All the more reason for making Finn and the Hexhunter's capture a priority," Eric growled.

Brenna's eyes bounced between the adults. "So you're going to do nothing? You're just going to allow a traitor to roam Midgard freely?"

"We have no conclusive proof you were kidnapped. It is more likely you are in league with Finn," Malin said.

"What?" Brenna couldn't believe what she was hearing.

Onem agreed. "We have your word and your word alone that you were kidnapped. For all we know, you *could* be conspiring with Finn."

"I'm giving you my word as a Witch of Folklore. That should be enough," Brenna said through clenched teeth.

Malin drew to her full height. "It is not." Her eyes narrowed like they were trying to penetrate Brenna's mind, searching for something and not finding it. "Let me remind you that aiding the renegade and her Hexhunter against the good of Folklore carries severe consequences—even execution."

"Lothar!" Brenna turned and pointed at him. "He was in the Hex's lair when Sarah freed me. Tell them."

All eyes fell on the prince. He cringed at the power of their collective stares. "I saw Sarah open a chest and Brenna appeared," he whispered meekly. Then, glancing at his father, he added, "But I have no actual proof she was kidnapped last night."

"You spineless *veslingr*!" Brenna lunged, her arms reaching for Lothar's throat. Haakon caught her and pulled her back. "You know it's true. You know Hel came to Midgard last night. No wonder Sarah punched you in the face. First chance I get, I'll do the same."

She tugged loose of the Jarl's grip and exited the room before anyone could see her tears.

Before stomping out of earshot, she heard Onem say, "You'll have to forgive her, Wicca. The girl has anger issues—just like her mother…"

Chapter 8

Grayle and Sarah reached the Hagia Sophia's central nave, a massive area beneath the museum's great dome. Measuring almost sixty feet across, the dome rested on four arches with forty windows circling its base. Rays of afternoon sunlight streamed far above their heads, reflecting off golden mosaics and lighting up motes of dust. A 200-foot scaffold towered from the marble floor to the dome's ceiling. Preoccupied with finding Halfdan's runes, Grayle never noticed the hundreds of metal pipes criss-crossing together. Looking at it now, the scaffold reminded him of the world's largest jungle gym.

"This was too easy," Grayle said. "People have been searching for this rune fragment for centuries, and we made it look simple."

"Simple when you have a Hexhunter," Sarah reminded him.

True. Without his touch revealing the rest of Halfdan's graffiti, no one would have known the runes were there.

But how can that be?

From what he'd learned, Hexhunters were supposed to be immune to magic. So why did his touch *magically* reveal new runes? If anything, he should been snuffing them out.

Things to figure out another time, he told himself.

"This was where the lines intersected on the map," Sarah said. "The stone should be around here somewhere."

Grayle casually bent down, pretending to tie his shoelaces. He slid his fingernails along minute cracks separating each of the floor's grey flagstones. "Halfdan's clue said there would be a doorway. Maybe there's a latch or a hidden entrance. All we have to do is pry it open."

He placed his palm on the flagstone slabs, hoping he could expose more magical writing.

Nothing.

Sarah groaned. "I see it."

"You do? Where?" Grayle stood and followed her gaze. "I don't see anything."

Her eyes fixed on the dome two hundred feet above them. "It's there. Plastered into the ceiling. I can see its aura."

Grayle forgot her Auralex powers not only saw the spectral light of living things, but that of magical artifacts as well. "How do we get to it? Jump on a broomstick and fly?"

"Ha, ha," she said sarcastically. "Wands, broomsticks, and pointy hats are for storybooks. I'll have to climb."

Grayle noticed she'd suddenly gone pale, looking more nervous than usual.

"What's the matter?"

She pursed her lips. "I'm not very good with heights."

"Then let me go."

"How are you going to get the stone off the ceiling? With your hands?" Sarah slipped her bag from her shoulder and handed it to him. "*I* have to go."

She opened the Velcro flap, removed the miniature shield and slid it over her forearm.

"What am I supposed to do while you're gone?" he asked. Things didn't go so well the last time they parted ways. Sarah nearly became a Hex's main course, and Frost Giants had almost turned him into a Popsicle.

"You can keep an eye out for trouble," she said. "And wish me luck."

Grayle watched her hurry across the nave. No one paid her much attention, not even when she reached the scaffold's stairway. A drooping chain with a sign saying "Keep Out" in both Turkish and English seemed to be the only security in Sarah's way. She took one last look around, then stepped over the chain and disappeared behind a maze of metal girders.

Grayle scanned the remaining tourists and tour groups in the Hagia's grand gallery. *Keep an eye out for trouble,* he repeated to himself.

If he'd learned one thing from his exposure to all things Folklore, it was that trouble could be disguised as anything or anyone—perhaps the museum guide leading Japanese tourists from one curiosity to the next, or the security guard at the southern exit, glancing at his watch, waiting for his shift to end. Maybe even the little girl having a tantrum, complaining about being bored. Hel could be shapeshifted into any one of them.

Grayle tapped his foot nervously, fidgeting with Sarah's bag strap. Alone in the middle of the nave, he realized *he* was the one coming across as awkward and out of place.

Focus, he told himself. *Keep an eye out for trouble, but look like a tourist.*

He sauntered to a collection of maps showing the Hagia Sophia's evolution from a third century Christian church to a twenty-first century museum. He glanced over his shoulder. Sarah was making good progress, moving almost cat-like up the stairs.

A family stood at the edge of the nave. The mom and dad pointed to one of the many round plaques with gold Arabic lettering suspended from the Hagia Sophia's ceiling. Their son and daughter playfully pushed and shoved one another behind them. Grayle had often thought how cool it would be to have a brother or sister…or one of each. Finding his parents was one thing, but the possibility of having a sibling excited him even more. Would the Eye be able to show him that too?

Another reason to find the relic before anyone else.

But first he and Sarah had to get this runestone, then somehow find the other two, and *then* steal the markers Caine and Hel already had.

A sinking feeling filled the pit of his stomach. *If Caine and Hel are working together, they'd have the resources of a billionaire and the magic of a goddess. It'd be almost impossible to—*

The ground suddenly lurched beneath his feet.

At first Grayle thought he'd stepped on a loose flagstone, momentarily losing his balance. Then the ground shook again, more violently this time, rocking back and forth with so much force he had to brace himself against the nearest wall.

Grayle had anticipated trouble, but he never expected it to be an earthquake.

Chapter 9

Brenna paced the corridor outside Onem's laboratory, still too furious to go back inside.

"Bunch of dungas," she muttered under her breath. *They'd rather chase Sarah than admit a more serious problem existed, like a traitor in Midgard.*

Onem, Haakon, and the Wicca didn't believe her kidnapping story, which meant no one would be looking for who let Hel into the city.

Finding the traitor will be left to me, she realized.

Voices from inside the lab drew closer.

Brenna slinked around the corner, keeping out of sight. She caught her breath when she saw Svein slumped against the wall. She'd forgotten he was ordered to stay behind.

His head drooped to one side—sleeping.

Brenna rolled her eyes. *And he's supposed to be my protector?*

"A warrant has been issued for Sarah Finn's arrest," she overheard Onem say. "With any luck, she will be apprehended in the next day or so."

"What of the Hexhunter?" Erik grumbled.

Malin's answer came out cold and harsh. "He must be eliminated. I will dispatch agents immediately."

"Where will you send them?"

"To the *capitals of the east*, of course. We will flush out the renegade and make sure…"

Their voices trailed off as they walked farther down the corridor.

Brenna pressed her back against the wall and let out a long, slow breath. *I have to get word to Sarah—fast.* Wherever she was, she needed to know what was happening. But how? No doubt Malin would intercept any outgoing communications, especially from her. Every vapor message Brenna made, every phone call, every bifrost destination would have a tracer spell on it.

She spotted Svein's cell phone clutched in his hand.

Would everyone's communications be monitored? she wondered.

She tip-toed over and carefully slipped the device from his grip.

The boy grunted, repositioned himself, and continued snoring.

Brenna worked fast, opening the phone's operating system. Using the latest encryption coding, she scrambled the phone's ID signature, set a fake caller ID, and wove a detracer spell of her own. She also set an alarm in case a tracer spell detected her call.

Brenna pressed her lips together. *It's the best I can do.*

She gambled on the Coven not having the same technical know-how as teenage magickers. But if she was wrong, if Malin somehow localized the call and found out who sent it…

Then I'll be the one branded a traitor.

She tapped out Sarah's number anyway and listened to dead air as her call transferred. A click. Two long beeps. Then the phone began to ring.

Chapter 10

Sarah focused on stealth over speed as she hiked up the metal scaffold. The soft clang of her sneakers was almost imperceptible. Painted safety orange, the steps zig-zagged to the top, helping restoration teams reach even the most inaccessible areas of the old dome. Lucky for her, there weren't any workmen in sight.

Halfway up, she made the mistake of looking down. Her stomach clenched instantly. She was already high enough to make every pore on her skin begin to sweat and her breathing to grow shallow. Most people had a phobia of some kind. Hers just happened to be acrophobia—the fear of heights.

Lightheaded, Sarah closed her eyes. *Have. To. Relax,* she told herself.

Bzzzt. Bzzzt. Bzzzt.

Her phone buzzed in her pocket. Three sharp bursts.

Emergency.

Sarah fished the device from her pocket and answered. She was surprised to see someone other than Grigsby on the screen. "Brenna? What's going on? How did you get this number?"

The blonde witch's bruised face stared back at her. "Nevermind that. I have to talk fast. Someone might be tracing our call."

"Why would someone trace—"

"No time to explain." Her voice radiated frustration. "Where are you? No, wait—don't tell me. It's best if I don't know." She looked somewhere off camera. "Sarah, Wicca Malin is in Midgard. The Coven's put a warrant out for your arrest. It won't be long until every Folklore has your face plastered in the streets."

Sarah swallowed. She was afraid this would happen. "What did they say about Grayle?"

Brenna bit her lip. "They want him dead, but they're not advertising it…for obvious reasons."

Sarah understood. Openly revealing Grayle's existence meant telling others that the Hexhunters may have returned. The news would ignite panic throughout Folklore.

"You have to lay low," Brenna warned.

"Hard to do when I'm trying to find an artifact that can destroy the world."

Sarah glanced at the runestone's aura glowing eighty feet above. Looking at it now, she was reminded of the utter devastation it could bring. If Hel got her hands on the runestones, and then the Eye, she'd use its power to learn how to release her father, Loki. The end result would be Ragnarok, gods battling monsters with helpless Outlanders and Folklorians stuck in the middle.

Sarah pursed her lips and brought the phone back to face level. "Have you found the traitor in Midgard?" she asked.

The other girl shook her head. "They don't even believe it happened." A warning chime pinged. "Dammit. I'm being traced. I gotta go before they find out I called you."

"Take care of yourself, Brenna."

"You too."

Sarah returned the phone to her pocket and resumed her climb.

It had been her decision not to inform the Coven about Grayle and her discovery of another piece of Mimir's Stone. She wasn't sure how Grayle fit into the search for the Eye, only that his proximity, his touch, seemed to directly affect all things linked to the artifact. She doubted the Coven or Wicca Malin would listen to her about all this.

Best thing to do is get the runestone and ask for forgiveness later, she thought. *Then at least we'd have something to bargain with.*

A knot twisted her stomach as she reached the scaffold's topmost platform.

Keep it together, she told herself, fighting off dizziness.

She warily approached the platform's railing and examined the partial runestone peeking through layers of stucco. It would have been concealed forever if the museum hadn't been in the process of restoring the dome. The surrounding plaster and cement holding the stone in place seemed brittle enough. It wouldn't take much to loosen it. She had to hurry. The longer she stayed, the greater chance she had of being discovered.

Propping her waist precariously on the top railing, she reached up with one hand.

"Rauco-balan."

A faint static charge zapped from her fingers, crossing the two yards between her and the imbedded stone. The spell had been one of the first she'd learned, teaching her how to use the surrounding ambient energy to create electricity. It was also a quick way to charge her iPod. Little by little, her magic chipped away at the plaster. Debris dropped to the floor two hundred feet below. Sarah hoped it would go unnoticed but didn't dare look down to find out. It didn't take long for the runestone's edges to take shape.

Odd. It doesn't match the one we found in Vancouver.

Unable to bear the stone's weight any longer, the remaining plaster suddenly broke away.

The fragment plummeted.

Sarah thrust out her arm. "Toltha!"

The stone halted in mid-air. Using every ounce of concentration, she willed the fragment to reverse course. It floated up to her outstretched hand.

Arms shaking, Sarah hauled the fragment over the railing. Her heart sank as she inspected her prize. Despite its aura, it wasn't the runestone they were searching for. For one, it wasn't carved on obsidian—black volcanic glass. It was a piece of granite. The runes looked hastily scrawled too, not in the same careful script as the others.

Commotion from below shifted Sarah's attention. A scream followed.

That was her cue to get out of there.

"Cidinn."

With a flash of blue magic, the stone shrank to the size of a pebble.

No sooner had Sarah tucked it into her pants pocket when a shockwave rippled up the scaffolding. The tremor bucked her off her feet. The platform lurched heavily to one side. Sarah slid toward the edge, grabbing the safety railing before going over completely. Heart pounding, her legs thrashed about in open air. Her arms strained as she swung her body, gaining enough momentum to hook a foot on the railing and pull herself up. She laid on the cold platform for a moment, heart beating like a jackhammer.

Tourists fled the nave far below, dodging falling debris.

Then Sarah spotted three draugr—the Viking equivalent of zombies. They scurried up the scaffolding like cockroaches toward her.

Sarah pursed her lips.

Trapped—with only one exit.

Down.

A long way down.

Chapter 11

To the casual eye, the tourists ambling along the Hagia Sophia's grounds were just that—tourists.

But the Operative knew better.

Disguised as a security guard, he'd been studying the sightseers on his way into the museum. Some trailed after tour guides babbling excitedly about the history surrounding them, while others preferred to bury their noses in guide books. Several took selfies, their faces blocking the attractions they intended to photograph. Others still favored sitting peacefully, taking in the wonders in quiet reflection.

Then five men caught his eye. At first they appeared no different from other tourists—until one looked closer. The broad shoulders, close-cropped hair. The tense, braced expressions. The secret glances directed at one another.

As if waiting for a signal, the Operative noted.

He tracked their movements for the next fifteen minutes. Sure enough, one of them raised a hand to a tiny device lodged in his ear.

Amateurs, the Operative thought. *No doubt mercenaries hired by Sebastian Caine. Who else would be tracking the two teenagers?*

He watched as the five men fanned out and entered the Hagia Sophia at thirty second intervals. The last of them remained at the museum's entrance. A sentry—stationed to keep guard.

The Operative moved swiftly, cutting his way through the crowd. Whoever these men were, they needed to be neutralized.

The mercenary left watching the entrance focused on people exiting the museum, not those coming in.

Another rookie mistake.

The Operative crept within three yards. He was about to subdue the lone sentry when the ground began to shake. People looked around, checking to see if others had felt the same tremor. A brick smashed to the ground a few feet away, narrowly missing a couple pushing a baby stroller. Confusion quickly turned to panic. A scream erupted from inside the museum. One at first, then two—three—a dozen. A moment later, visitors came pouring out of the building like ants abandoning a nest.

Taking advantage of the confusion, the Operative darted forward and wrapped a beefy forearm around the sentry's neck. He squeezed, cutting off the man's blood and oxygen supply to the brain. The mercenary struggled, flailing his arms in a vain attempt to escape. Then his weight sagged in the Operative's arms.

Out cold.

The Operative dragged him behind a pillar, removed the man's earpiece, and placed it in his own.

"Alpha, the witch is on the scaffold," came a crackled voice.

"Nevermind her. Get the kid," a different voice ordered.

"Sir, we have Zs in the central nave," said a third.

Zs—Zombies.

The Operative slid a baton from his belt and hurried inside.

Chapter 12

The earthquake rumbled through the old church like a passenger jet. Plaster chips cracked and windows shattered. Chandeliers swayed like pendulums. Tourists froze, their brains unable to make sense of the vibrations below their feet. Then, like a switch being thrown, they scrambled over one another, racing for the exits. Some lost their balance and were reduced to crawling on hands and knees. Others curled into the fetal position, paralyzed by fear.

Grayle's first instinct wasn't to flee but to find Sarah...make sure she was alright. He searched the scaffold. By the time he noticed the draugr, it was too late. The zombies had reached the metal tower, climbing the pipeworks to get to her. One had already reached the top.

She needs my help.

He forced himself to let go of the wall and move against the desperate flow of tourists. Another tremor sent him stumbling into four men blocking his path. Odd, neither of the four made an effort to flee the museum or duck for cover. They stood where they were, rigid, eying him like prey. It took Grayle a moment to realize they were here for him.

A baton appeared in one of the men's hands like a horrible magic trick. More than a baton—electricity fizzled blue at the end of the weapon. It was a Taser stick. He launched forward, jabbing the stick at Grayle's chest. Before Grayle knew what he was doing, he sidestepped and grabbed the man's arm. He followed by kicking the legs out from under his attacker as if he'd done it a thousand times. The man crashed heavily onto the marble floor. Without stopping, Grayle twisted his arm and buried the baton's sizzling end into the man's stomach. His attacker flopped like a fish as fifty thousand volts coursed through his body. Then he went still.

Grayle barely had enough time to process what he'd done before the next attacker aimed a Taser gun at him. The floor pitched as the man pulled the trigger. Grayle stumbled, and the two wired electrodes zipped past, electrifying empty air. Regaining his balance, Grayle aimed a fierce kick at the shooter's solar plexus. His heel drove into the man's stomach. The attacker cried out, and the Taser fell sparking to the ground. Next, Grayle landed an elbow to his neck. The man grunted and went down hard.

Grayle stumbled back. *What was that?*

His counterattacks came like a reflex. He'd never had that kind of close quarters combat training before. Sure, he'd been in fights—quite a few, in fact—but what he did just now went beyond anything he thought he was capable of.

Fearing his luck wouldn't last, Grayle turned to run. He rushed straight into a barrel-chested man wearing a dark suit. It was like walking into a brick wall. He looked up and saw Nils Mussels' beady eyes glaring down at him. Grayle tried to twist his body for another karate kick, but it was too late. The bodyguard's great, meaty hands closed around his throat.

"We meet again, runt," Mussels said. The veiny muscles in his neck bulged as he spoke. "Do you remember what I said to you in Baldersted?"

Grayle wasn't sure. He recalled a bunch of things, like the bodyguard shooting tranquilizer darts at him and then threatening to twist his head off like a bottle cap.

"I said I would rather kill you than give you to Monsieur Caine. *Je suis satisfait* I have this opportunity again."

Although people were still inside the Hagia Sophia, no one would notice the 300-pound bodyguard manhandling a teenager; the earthquake saw to that. No one was going to come to his aid.

In an act of desperation, he punched Mussels in the jaw.

The man never even flinched.

Defeated, there was nothing left to do but give up. Grayle felt his body sag. His pulse throbbed in his neck. He saw spots in front of his eyes.

He was blacking out.

Chapter 13

Sarah shot to her feet, scanning for a way to get off the scaffold alive and in one piece. On either side of the nave were two access passages running the length of the building. Above these were another two corridors lined with colonnades. The closest was thirty feet away.

What am I going to do?

At that moment, the first draug heaved onto the platform. Draped in torn clothing and cracked leather armor, he leered at Sarah with clouded eyes. He pulled out a double-bladed axe laced to his back. Despite the zombie's decrepit appearance, Sarah knew he had the strength to cleave her in two.

With a growl, the draug came at her, swinging. The axe sliced downward. Sarah jumped out of the way and threw a backfist. The miniaturized shield, still strapped to her forearm, bashed into the zombie's face. An eyeball and several teeth went flying.

Too bad the undead didn't feel pain.

The zombie thrust his axe handle to the right. The butt dug into Sarah's ribs. She stumbled back, gasping for air. Shifting his stance, the draug one-handed the weapon and delivered a cross swing that would have lopped Sarah's head from her shoulders. She ducked in time. Before the zombie could attack again, she conjured her pulse spell.

"Vanya!"

An invisible wave caught the creature square in the chest, hurling him against the opposite railing. With a sickening crack, the draug's spine snapped in half. He fell on the scaffold landing. But even a broken back didn't stop him. The draug crawled toward her, teeth gnashing, bony fingers clawing the metal platform. Decapitation or incineration were the only ways to stop a draug for good.

Sarah picked up the axe. She pressed her foot into his back, holding him down.

"Go back to Helheim and be at peace."

She chopped down. Both head and body dissolved into a heap of fine gray powder that trickled through the landing's grate. Whoever the draug had been in life, he would never be among the living dead again.

Another jolt rocked the scaffold, vibrating so hard it made Sarah's teeth chatter. She let go of the axe and clung to the railing as the tower teetered from side to side. Pipes broke loose somewhere farther down, tumbling to the floor. Their hollow clangs sounded like church bells. With a terrible shearing, the frame crumpled, and the whole scaffold began toppling over. Sarah screamed. Her feet slipped from the landing as gravity shifted, turning her world perilously on its side. She imagined the entire framework coming apart like a Jenga tower. With a metallic screech, the top of the scaffold scraped along the dome, sending chunks of plaster, brick and mortar falling. Then, wedging into the topmost arch, the tower shuddered to a stop.

Sarah gasped for breath. Her heart hammered in her chest. Dangling from the railing, she looked at the twisted metal below her. The stairs were a mangled mess. One of the pursuing draug had gotten pinned between several collapsed metal girders. The last draug remained unscathed. His limbs twisted at unnatural angles, weaving in and out of the piping, getting closer.

More supports began to buckle, stretching and tearing from the pressure. They stripped from the rest of the scaffold like a peeling banana and crashed into the church's brickwork. Several fell across the nave and smashed onto the parapet to Sarah's left. She spotted a pipe only a few yards below, slanted toward the adjacent passageway.

I can use it to shimmy across, she thought. It had the right angle and direction. *It might work.*

Sarah gritted her teeth. The will to survive replaced her fear of heights. She reached for the next closest handhold and clambered down, using the piping like monkey bars. The metal tubes creaked and groaned under her weight, threatening to come apart.

The phone in her pocket vibrated, chiming the old western movie tune *The Good, The Bad, and The Ugly.* Grigsby's ringtone.

"Not now," she said, carefully negotiating her next grip and foothold.

Arriving at the pipe stretching the length of the nave, Sarah saw it was too narrow to balance on.

What am I going to do? I'm no tightrope walker—and if another tremor comes while I'm on it...

Nerves clenched her stomach again. It was still a long way to fall.

There was one other option. Her shield.

Sarah acted quickly. She swung her legs up, hooking them on a different pipe. With her hands free, she slid the shield from her forearm.

"Ga'la."

The shield grew to normal size. Sarah slung it over the slanted pipe. The plan was to use the shield and slide across to the colonnade. Hanging by the leather wrist straps, she let out a squeak and was about to unhook her foot from the scaffold when something grabbed her ankle.

Sarah gasped. The last draug clung to her leg, preventing her escape. She twisted and managed to kick the zombie hard in the face. The impact broke his jaw and wrenched his neck a full one eighty degrees, but it wasn't enough to turn the creature to dust. Switching tactics, Sarah kicked at the zombie's arm. Once—twice—the third strike snapped the brittle appendage off.

Free of the draug's grip, the shield scraped along the pipe like a zipline, carrying Sarah over the gap between the scaffold and second level colonnade. She feared that at any moment its leather handles would rip or that her dangling weight would snap the shield in half. Both scenarios would have fatal results. Sarah tried not to think about it. The parapet was approaching fast—too fast—but there was no way to slow her descent. She lifted her legs, ready to cushion the impact.

Then another tremor shook the museum.

The pipe she was sliding on buffeted and shifted angles. Sarah screamed. Her forward motion stopped as the direction changed. Now she was plunging backward, back toward the scaffolding, back toward the draug. Unable to see where she was going, Sarah prepared for a bone-jarring collision. It never came. Instead, she felt the zombie's sinewy arm wrap around her neck, pinning her in place. Sarah twisted and strained to pull free, all the while trying to keep her head from being bitten. She liked her brains where they were. But the draug made no move to feed his appetite. Sarah wondered why.

The answer came in the form of a rising shadow as black as a starless night. The shadow solidified into a cloak billowing like the wings of a demon. A face, conjured from the depths of Sarah's nightmares, materialized next—half-human, half rotting skeleton.

Hel—the goddess of death.

"Give me the stone, witch," she hissed. A trail of burning brimstone fluttered in her wake.

"I don't have it," Sarah yelled back. She glanced below. No one noticed the cloaked figure levitating eighty feet in the air, or the girl being held against the scaffolding like a fly caught in a spider's web.

"You are lying."

"I'm not. The stone in the ceiling was a decoy."

The goddess's eyes smoldered neon green. She let out a frustrated screech. "Do not toy with me, witchling."

"I swear, I don't have it!"

Hel's face twitched. "You must give it to me. It is for the good of us all."

"The good of us all? Are you kidding me? How stupid do you think I am?" Sarah winced as the draug tightened his grip around her throat. "You'll use the stone to bring about Ragnarok. How is that the good for us all?"

"You've been deceived, witchling. The Coven will never let you reach the Eye. They are hunting for you at this very moment."

How did she know?

The goddess must have seen the look in Sarah's eyes. "I am right then." Hel smirked, or what looked like a smirk when one only had half a face. "Give me the runestone," she said again. "You don't know what you are meddling in. No mortal can withstand the Eye's power. It is useless to you."

There was an almost pleading, sincere quality in her tone.

Was she telling the truth? Does she actually think she's helping?

Sarah shook her head. "For the last time, I don't have it. And even if I did, I'd never give it to *you*."

The hem of Hel's cloak floated toward her. Like tendrils made of dark mist, they stroked Sarah's cheek. It was cold, like being caressed by fingers made of ice. The chill sank through Sarah's skin, down to her very soul. The darkness, the despair…

"If you do not give me what I want willingly," Hel continued, "I can always turn you into one of them." Her gaze fixed on the draug over Sarah's shoulder.

As if on cue, the zombie groaned in her ear. It reeked of rancid meat.

Sarah gagged at the foul stench. "I. Don't. Have. The runestone."

"A draug it is, then." Hel floated closer, her arm extended. The silver gauntlet, etched with the runes of Helheim, inched toward Sarah's throat.

Sarah held her breath so as not to choke on the brimstone fumes. She squirmed under the zombie's grip. Black tentacles spread over her. She tried to scream, but the cries were absorbed as darkness enveloped her.

Chapter 14

The Operative pushed past panicked tourists, racing to intercept the mercenaries. If the mercs got to the Hexhunter first, there was no telling what they'd do. Kidnap, maim, murder him?

Whatever their intent, he wasn't going to let it happen.

Reaching the central nave, he took in the scene. Civilians huddled beside marble pillars, thinking they were safe under the arches and supports. Plaster chunks and other debris littered the museum floor. A massive scaffold erected at the far end of the dome looked ready to collapse. Amid the bent metal piping, the Operative picked out a single figure being held against the pipeworks.

The witch.

Hel floated like a black mist across from her.

The Operative's orders were clear: No harm was to come to the Hexhunter. The witch, if necessary, was expendable.

She'll have to fend for herself.

He switched his attention to the nave floor, spotting the remaining mercenaries converging on the Hexhunter like a pack of hungry wolves.

Without the benefit of stealth or surprise, the Operative knew the odds were stacked against him. He charged headlong into the fray anyway, letting his training and experience take over.

One of the mercenaries spotted his approach. He pointed a Taser gun.

The Operative swung his baton before the man could aim. The merc cried out as the hardened plastic caught his wrist. The Taser clattered to the floor. The Operative spun, throwing an elbow at the man's head. The impact knocked him senseless.

Using his forward momentum, the Operative charged at his next adversary. The second mercenary was more prepared, kicking the baton from the Operative's hand. The merc went to follow up with a straight jab to the face. The Operative hooked the attacker's arm under his own. He punched the man in the jaw and shoulder flipped him to the floor, before delivering a final knockout punch.

The Operative looked up. *Where were the other two?*

He watched as the Hexhunter bent low and swept his leg just above his attacker's knee. The mercenary toppled, cracking his head on the stone floor.

Remarkable. The boy was fending them off, moving with more strength and agility than the Operative thought possible.

Some kind of inherent skill?

One had to wonder.

Then a hulking shadow emerged behind the Hexhunter like an eclipse. Nils Mussels rushed out from a nearby pillar and clamped his hands on the boy's shoulders. The bodyguard delivered a knee strike to the Hexhunter's stomach.

The Operative drew his Sig Sauer from his uniform jacket. Standard Crusader issue. Efficient. Ruthless. He aimed, but thought against firing. One more unannounced tremor, one slight shift or miscalculation, and he could shoot the boy. He picked up a fallen stun baton instead. Twirling it into a throwing grip, he aimed for Mussels' head and threw.

Chapter 15

Grayle was vaguely aware of something hurdling through the air.

With a dull *thwack*, Mussels' head snapped back, and his grip around Grayle's neck loosened. Like a trapped animal sensing escape, Grayle wriggled free and staggered away. Gasping for air, he peeked over his shoulder. The Belgian Brawler had collapsed onto the floor and was struggling to get back up.

Grayle knew he didn't have much time before Mussels shook off whatever had brought him down. He rushed to what was left of the scaffolding. The metal tower leaned precariously to one side. The top propped against the lower edge of the dome, threatening to come apart at any moment.

"Sarah!"

He spotted her splayed against the metal frame, held in place by a draug. Hel floated in a cloud of burning brimstone across from her, closing in with one hand reaching out to grab Sarah's throat.

What can I do? What can I do? Grayle searched around frantically for anything that could help. All he saw was chaos. Flower-shaped chandeliers swayed from the ceiling. Pipes, severed from the scaffold, lay scattered on the floor like pick-up sticks. People huddled under arches and in far corners, refusing to move, fearing another tremor could bring more debris raining down on them.

A security guard stood ten yards away. He, too, was focused on Hel hovering eighty feet in the air. His hand reached into his uniform jacket and came out holding a gun with a thick silencer attached to its barrel.

That can't be standard issue, Grayle thought.

Straight-arming the weapon, the guard aimed and fired. One by one, the bullets found their mark, slicing into Hel's robes like hot knives through butter.

The Death Queen shrieked. Trails of smoke seeped from where the bullets had torn into her body. She convulsed, jerking and twitching. An invisible force was pulling her inside herself until she disappeared into oblivion.

Grayle stared open-mouthed.

The security guard tucked the gun back in his jacket. For a split second, their eyes met.

Grayle had seen those eyes before, but where?

He started moving toward the guard when the draug who'd been holding Sarah bounced off the girders. The creature burst into ashes seconds after smacking onto the stone floor.

Looking up, Grayle saw Sarah hanging from the pipes, trying to find a better handhold to pull herself up.

When Grayle looked back, the guard had vanished. *Where did he go? Why'd he take off?*

"Don't move, Hexhunter!" a voice warned behind him.

Grayle froze, lifting both arms. He turned slowly and faced a man wearing an expensive black, tailored suit. Grayle recognized him instantly. A trimmed goatee, long white hair slicked back into a ponytail, and, despite sunglasses hiding his eyes, an expression of deep satisfaction.

It was Sebastian Caine, aiming a gun at Grayle's head.

Not a Taser—a real gun.

* * *

Sarah stared at the empty space in front of her. One moment the Death Queen was hovering toward her, the next she was folding in on herself like crumpled paper, imploding into nothingness.

What happened? Was she dead? *Can't be. It would take a lot more to kill a—*

The draug's bony arm tightened around her throat, a reminder she wasn't out of danger yet. Sarah grabbed the desiccated limb with both hands.

"Naur-galad."

The incineration spell burned into the zombie's dried-out skin. It smoldered at first, then burst into flames, which spread from his forearm to his shoulder in a matter of seconds. Sarah grabbed hold of a pipe above and tore herself free, taking a piece of the creature's charred arm with her.

On fire and with nothing to hold on to, the draug tumbled from the scaffold and disintegrated into dust as he hit the Hagia Sophia's slab floor.

Sarah let out a collected breath. She'd come close to death before, but not like that.

Time to find Grayle and get out of here.

She spotted him below with his arms raised. A man pointed a gun at him.

Not just any man.

Fury spread through Sarah's body like wildfire.

It was Sebastian Caine.

Her eyes sharpened.

The plan to zipline across to the parapet already forgotten, she hooked an arm around the pipe she'd been holding and pulled her shield free. "Cidinn." It shrunk to the size of a Frisbee.

A chain holding one of the Hagia Sophia's many chandeliers hung ten feet away from where she balanced. Without a second thought, Sarah let go of the scaffolding and flung herself across the empty space. Her body soared. She reached, hands flailing to where the chain should have been.

Nothing.

Panic jolted her. She was going to fall to her death.

Then her fingers brushed metal.

Instantly, the pain of witch on iron seared her flesh. The metal links burned cruelly into her palms. Her shoulders screamed, the bones nearly ripping from their sockets. Arm muscles burning, she slid down a hundred feet, hitting the chandelier with so much force it broke loose from its anchors in the ceiling.

Both witch and chandelier plunged to the floor.

* * *

Normally, Grayle would have been more afraid having a gun pointed at his head, but his experiences in the last forty-eight hours had increased his tolerance for fear. He didn't know what he could do to save himself anyway. Moments ago he was able to take out two adult attackers, using a mix of skills and strength he never knew he had. But he couldn't beat a bullet. He wasn't Superman.

"What do you want from me?" Grayle asked.

A smirk spread across the billionaire's face. The last time Grayle had seen that grin was in the Vancouver Museum, when Caine welcomed dignitaries, movie stars, and honored guests to "The Mysteries of the Vikings" exhibit.

"I want what you can give me," the billionaire replied. His smirk vanished, replaced by a callous scowl.

"Which is?" Grayle asked. He was sure Caine was going to say "to get the Eye of Odin."

The billionaire answered with a single word: "Justice."

Grayle's brows knit together. "Justice? How can I—"

His question was cut short by a sharp, metallic clink.

Something fell from the sky.

Grayle moved without thinking, hurling himself out of the path of a plummeting chandelier. Caine was taken by surprise. The billionaire stumbled backward. On purpose or not, he managed to fire off a single shot before losing his grip on the gun. The bullet went nowhere near Grayle, disappearing somewhere into the Hagia's plaster walls.

The chandelier crashed with the violent sound of shattering glass and crushing metal.

When Grayle looked back, he saw Sarah standing among the chandelier's twisted brass.

She did not look happy.

Chapter 16

The crash landing rattled Sarah's bones, almost throwing her off the chandelier. She clung to the fixture's neck tube at the last second and managed to hold on. She glared at Caine, her mother's killer lying there helpless, leg pinned under the smashed metal. The impact had sent his gun sliding across the floor. All she had to do was finish it, get the revenge she'd been craving. She balled her fists and shakily climbed from the heap of broken lights.

Caine squirmed, trying to free himself from the wreckage.

There's nowhere to hide, murderer. You're mine.

All that time she could have spent with her mother was lost forever, because of this man.

Grayle scrambled to his feet and blocked her path. "Are you crazy? What do you think you're doing?"

Sarah grabbed him by the shirt collar. "Stay out of this, Grayle! This is between me and him!"

He refused to back away. "What are you going to do…kill him?"

She could feel hot tears gathering behind her eyes. She had plenty of rage to purge. She didn't need Grayle getting in the way.

"Sarah, killing him won't bring your mom back."

She took another step forward.

"You need to calm down."

A terrible tug-of-war waged inside her. What was she doing? She knew she couldn't kill the man. She wanted to—boy, did she want to—but to cross that line…it would be going too far.

She forced herself to relax.

Grayle looked over her shoulder. "We need to get out of here. Now!"

Mussels and four men were pulling themselves off the floor. They shed their civilian clothing, revealing black military fatigues underneath.

Sarah recognized the silver crosses stitched to their shirts.

Crusaders.

Grayle pulled her in the direction of the exit. They rushed along a corridor leading back to the atrium. They were cut off by their tour guide.

"Not that way," Nazan said. "Come with me."

Grayle was about to follow when Sarah held him back. "How do we know we can trust you?" she asked. "We don't know anything about you." For all they knew, she could be in league with Caine or Hel—or a Roman agent.

"Because I am the only chance you have at getting out of here," she said. "And it appears you don't have a choice."

The Crusaders burst into the far end of the corridor, spotting them.

Nazan was right. What was the alternative? They didn't know how many more of Caine's henchmen could be waiting outside.

They followed the girl down a nave going deeper *into* the Hagia Sophia.

"Where are you taking us?" Grayle asked.

Nazan pushed open a heavy wooden door marked "Sadece Yetkili Personel"—Authorized Personnel Only.

"There's a better way out of here," she said, quickly ushering them inside.

Hinges creaked as Sarah pushed the door shut behind them. She slid a thick beam across the handles, then hurried after Grayle and the tour guide down a dimly lit corridor. Five modern office doors, equally spaced apart, lined the wall to her left. Turkish writing labeled the frosted glass. Nazan unlocked the last door, and they slipped inside. The room held a jumble of gear and equipment. It was dominated by a large metal table with several tools used to clean and reassemble mosaic pieces scattered on its surface.

Nazan hurried past the table, focusing on a brick wall to their right.

A loud thump-thump echoed from the hallway.

"They're coming," Grayle warned.

Nazan slid both hands along the wall's rough surface, searching for something.

"Whatever you're doing, do it faster," Sarah told her.

With a loud crack, a shock of light penetrated the frosted window. Multiple shadows moved down the hallway outside. Sarah heard footsteps, followed by hushed voices. Another crash came a moment later.

"They're kicking in the office doors, looking for us," Grayle whispered.

A second crash.

A sick feeling roiled in Sarah's gut. Their room had no exit, other than the way they came in.

Third crash.

She moved to the end of the long metal table. "Grayle, help me." Bits of mosaic bounced as they pushed the table, using it to barricade the office door.

Fourth crash.

"How much magic you got left?" Grayle asked nervously.

She concentrated, trying to connect with the ambient energy. Icy needles prickled her skin. The magic traveled through her veins to the tips of her fingers. But instead of the inferno she felt minutes ago, she could only muster a dull burn. "Not much," she said.

Shadows emerged outside their window. A sturdy kick crashed into the door, shifting the table and cracking the frosted glass. Sharp commands followed. The Crusaders knew they'd found them.

This is it. Sarah glanced over her shoulder. Nazan was still at the far side of the wall, pressing different bricks. Without a way to escape, they would have to stand and fight.

The next powerful kick shattered the glass and pushed the table farther from the door.

Sarah timed her attack. "Naur-galad!"

Before the Crusaders had a chance to aim their weapons, she tossed a fireball through the broken window, singing the lead Crosser in the chest. Shouts of surprise followed.

"Found it!" Nazan announced.

But Sarah was only half-listening as the sound of scraping stone rumbled behind her.

Like a charging bull, Mussels rammed the door, tearing it off its hinges. He grabbed the table blocking his way and flung it aside as if it were a plastic toy.

"Sarah! C'mon!" Grayle shouted.

A secret passage had opened, leaving a dark gap where the brick wall had been moments before.

Sarah backpedalled, chucked one last fireball to cover their escape, and stepped inside. Nazan smacked another brick as

Crossers stormed the room. More scraping, and the wall sealed shut between them. Everything went pitch black. Sarah heard scuffling on the opposite side of the wall. A man barked orders to find the switch that opened it.

"That won't stop them for long," Grayle said.

Nazan turned on her phone's flashlight app. "Long enough for us to get out of here."

She aimed the beam into the blackness, revealing a narrow shaft with brick arches. "This way. Hurry."

Hunched over, they crept through a maze of winding tunnels.

"Good thing we're not claustrophobic," Grayle muttered.

Space was tight. At times they barely had enough room, squirming sideways past chiseled stone or crawling on hands and knees. Sarah felt like she was squeezing down a serpent's throat, long and twisting.

It wasn't long before they reached another brick wall.

Nazan pulled a wooden lever, and a secret door swung open onto a wide chamber. The air reeked of stagnant water. Rows of columns climbed from a watery floor, supporting arches that held up the ceiling. Odd. The water appeared to be illuminated, as if it had a natural glow. It wasn't until Sarah looked closer that she saw lights submerged at the base of each column. Positioned upward, the lights spread eerie yellow-green shadows throughout the room.

"What is this place?" Grayle asked.

"The cisterns of Constantinople," Nazan answered, stepping down into the water. "They supplied water to much of the old city during ancient times."

Fish darted out of the way as they splashed through the ankle-deep water.

The cistern was empty. No doubt the earthquake that cleared the Hagia Sophia of tourists had done the same here.

Sarah's phone vibrated in her pocket.

Grigsby.

She had to let him know of their status. The call had to be short though. Thirty seconds, tops. Any longer and she risked exposing their location to anyone searching for her signal.

"Hey. We're alright," she said before the Caretaker could ask.

"What in tarnashin' happened?"

"Earthquake…and we had a little run-in with—" Sarah glanced at Nazan—"with others." She didn't want to divulge too much in front of her. "They may have been Crossers, but we're okay."

"Where're you headin'? I'll meet up with you."

"No. Go back to the *Drakkar* and keep her safe."

"But—"

"I'll contact you later. Trust me. Bye." She pressed End.

"We have to get topside and somewhere safe," Sarah said. "It won't take the Crossers long to figure out where the secret tunnel led to."

"This way." Nazan pointed toward the stairwell leading back up to the city streets. "I'll take you to my Folklore."

Chapter 17

Hel emerged inside the grand hall of her fortress in Helheim. The stronghold had been her home for countless millennia, ever since Odin gave her the distinction of becoming the goddess of death.

Gave?

She neither asked nor wanted the distinction. The position was demanded of her. Her grotesque appearance and being the daughter of Loki saw to that. Odin had cast her out of Asgard without a second thought. She fell for two days and two nights, landing in Niflheim, the coldest and darkest of the Nine Realms.

She staggered across the hall's black slate floor, keeping pressure on her wounds. Hel despised her palace, hating its eerie silence, the dead company, and its stark surroundings. She had tried to add color to it once—a red curtain here, a vibrant tapestry there. Within hours they had all turned to the same dusty gray as the rest of the fortress. It was as if Helheim not only sucked the life from one's soul, but the light and color of anything remotely uplifting.

She dragged herself up a flight of steps to where a single throne sat. Thrain, the captain of her draugr, stood next to it, waiting. He made no attempt to help his mistress as she grabbed the throne's armrest and plopped into the hard seat. Wisps of smoke drained from where the iron bullets punctured her body.

"The Outlanders grow bolder, your grace," Thrain said, handing her a chalice filled with mead. "Let me kill them for you, including the witch and boy."

Hel didn't ask how he knew an Outlander was responsible for her injuries. She drank from her cup, savouring the taste and letting the fermented liquid soothe her wounds. Its magical properties would help speed her recovery.

"I do not want them dead, you fool," she hissed. "Dead witches and Hexhunters are of no use to me."

Thrain was large for a zombie, suffering from the same afflictions as the rest of her dead minions: the clouded eyes, rotting skin, and missing teeth. But unlike many zombies his age, the rest of Thrain was mostly intact—including his tongue, which Hel had contemplated cutting out more than once. The captain had a tendency to offer opinions when they weren't welcome. Still, she kept him around. The alternative—eerie silence and no one to talk to—was more disturbing than the zombie captain's brash attitude.

"And you've allied yourself with a wealthy Outlander as well," Thrain said. The exposed sinewy flesh on his left cheek stretched and contracted as he spoke.

"I did."

"Never in a thousand years have you done such a thing, your grace. Why now?"

If Thrain was waiting for an explanation, he wasn't going to get one. She didn't need to explain her decisions—not to him, not to anyone.

"And what of your ally in Midgard?" he continued.

Hel grimaced, turning to find a more comfortable perch on her throne. Was he purposely trying her patience?

"He is no longer of use," she said. The traitor had done his part, managing to get her inside the forbidden city in order to stay close to the Hexhunter.

"But it is true…we have a way into Midgard?" the draug captain asked.

Despite her pain, Hel smirked and nodded. In his haste, the traitor failed to take into account the long-term consequences of his betrayal. A doorway into Midgard existed now, to be exploited at a later date. "Do not worry, Thrain. Your time will come," she said. Then, added coldly, "But you will do *what* you're told, *when* you're told. Remember that." She sipped her mead. "You're dismissed."

The draug bowed and left the hall.

Skoll and Manegarm pushed through the door Thrain had exited. They bounded into the hall, yipping and yowling like two newborn colts. Their singed fur was lit like glowing embers and smoke plumes scattered in their wake. The halls of Helheim may spoil the most vibrant colors, but it did little to tarnish the Helhounds' joy at seeing their mistress.

They brushed up against her.

"My babies."

Her hounds were the only source of affection she'd ever received. Her father was sent to purgatory soon after her exile from Asgard. The last she heard, he was strapped to a boulder and forced to endure a snake's venom steadily dripping into his eyes. Hel needed to free him. His salvation was linked to hers. But Loki's current location was a mystery. He was said to be in a region of Niflheim even beyond her reach. If she found a way to release him, her father would be able to take her from this place. She could start a new life, decide her own fate.

That's why finding the Eye of Odin was paramount. It would give her the information she needed. The freedom she craved.

"How do I proceed?" Hel muttered aloud, stroking Skoll's head.

The Hel-hound savored her attention as her metal fingers left blazing streaks in his fur.

Force and power seemed ineffective against the witch and Hexhunter. She was able to take the runestone from them in the Vancouver Museum days ago, but not without difficulty. The appearance of the Hexhunter had surprised her. Not even her magic could penetrate the boy's powers.

Was Thrain right? Would it be easier to kill them both and hunt for the runestone markers free of their meddling?

No. The Hexhunter was too important in the Eye of Odin's retrieval. The witchling, however, was expendable.

Or was she?

The bond between the girl and Hexhunter had grown stronger and faster than Hel anticipated.

Did they care for one another?

In her experience, bonds like that tended to be a burden, a weakness.

A weakness that can be exploited.

Then something occurred to her, something she should have exploited when she first encountered Sarah Finn in the Vancouver Museum.

Why use threats and intimidation when I can coerce the witchling another way?

"Babies."

Skoll and Manegarm lifted their massive heads, ears perked.

"I have a task for you."

The beasts shot to their feet; lava drooled from their snouts.

"Fetch me the ghost of Rachel Finn. Bring her to me."

Obeying her command, the Hel-hounds bolted from the hall.

Chapter 18

"You want to buy carpet, yes?"

The shopkeeper appeared in front of Grayle like a genie springing from a lamp.

"No, thanks," Grayle said, squeezing past him then ducking under a rolled up rug balanced on a man's shoulder.

He ran to catch up to Sarah and Nazan. Together, they snaked their way through a maze of passages inside Istanbul's famous Grand Bazaar. The vast marketplace covered sixty-one streets and contained three thousand shops. If Caine's mercenaries were in pursuit, they'd have a hard time finding them in these labyrinthine passageways. Tourists and locals bustled inside the market, staring into shop windows offering everything from jewellery and spices to carpets and linen. Waiters carried trays with little cups of espresso. Shopkeepers stood outside their storefronts, eager to draw in customers with money to spend.

Nazan ignored it all, knifing through the crowds. She peered over her shoulder occasionally, throwing Grayle the same concentrated look Sarah used to back in Bayview's hallways.

Crap. What if Nazan's an Auralex? What if she knows I'm a Hexhunter?

He leaned in closer to Sarah's ear. "Is she like you?" he asked.

"If you're asking me if she's a girl: yes, she is."

"I'm asking if she's an Auralex. She keeps looking at me weird."

Sarah sighed. "Back away and I'll take a look."

Grayle gave her space to use her Auralex senses.

Sarah's eyes strained and her face twitched. "No. You're safe," she concluded. "Maybe she's looking at you because—"

Sarah stopped and spun around. Something had spooked her.

"What's wrong?"

She started walking faster. "We have to hurry."

"What is it?" Grayle pressed.

She ignored him and fell in line with Nazan. "Is the entrance much farther?" she asked. Apparently the quickest route between the Hagia Sophia and Ottoman Folklore was through the bazaar.

Nazan pointed down an alley. "There it is."

They hurried to an unassuming arch spanning the width of the alley. Chipped and weathered from years of erosion, it looked older than the surrounding brickwork.

As they passed under the archway, a new city shimmered before Grayle's eyes. Buildings, practically stacked one on top of the other, swept up a gradual slope. Grayle could tell they'd once been decorated with bright designs, but the colors had faded, leaving a canvas of drab browns. Cracks zig-zagged up plaster walls, having grown longer and deeper over time. Sun-bleached banners hung from windows, dust-laden and frayed. Wind swirled dust funnels into corners where litter had gathered. Other than creaking signs moving in the breeze and the shrill cries of crows in the sky, the city was eerily quiet.

Grayle turned, wondering if anyone had noticed their crossing into the magical realm. *How can such a large part of the city remain hidden?* he thought. It boggled the mind. Wouldn't Google Earth spot it from orbit? Would birds disappear into the barrier and then reappear? Wouldn't anyone notice that?

Something to ask Sarah later.

A beggar, sitting with his back to a wall, reached out his bony palms. "Gıda. Lütfen, biraz yiyecek," he pleaded.

Whatever he was asking for, Grayle was sure he didn't have any to give. Neither did Sarah. Nazan paid him no attention whatsoever. She led them through a short tunnel that opened onto a wide courtyard. Hallways four storeys high faced the courtyard on all sides. Shrubbery neglected and on the verge of dying, bordered the enclosure. An elaborate fountain rose from the courtyard's center. The fountain was dry, reminding Grayle of how thirsty he was.

Nazan spread her arms. "This is home."

"It's nice. Peaceful," Sarah said.

"You are kind. Our Kingdom was once more beautiful. Our people much happier."

"What happened?" Grayle asked.

"The Romans. They've been advancing into our territory, using fear and intimidation to control key locations and our access to resources, like food and water."

"Why hasn't anyone heard of this?" Sarah asked. "The Coven needs to—"

"The Coven knows!" Nazan spat, suddenly bristling with anger. "They've known for some time…and have done nothing."

An awkward silence followed.

Nazan's shoulders sagged. "Sorry. I did not mean to lose my temper."

"No need to apologize," Sarah said. "Romans can be as prickly as a thorn bush. The Coven, too."

The corner of Nazan's mouth lifted. "To be honest, I thought you were Roman agents when I first saw you."

"We are travelers from Midgard," Sarah explained. "My name is Brenna Bjorndottir. This is Alistair."

Grayle's eyebrows shot up. *Alistair?*

"Nazan Mataraci. Why were you in the Hagia Sophia today? Why were you being attacked?"

Sarah shifted her feet nervously. "Maybe we can answer your questions a little later. Right now, we could use some rest."

Nazan's eyes narrowed. Grayle could tell it wasn't the answer she was looking for. "Of course. I will take you to one of our guest rooms."

She led them up a stairwell and along the third floor breezeway. The walls, made of smooth marble blocks, were bare except for the occasional painted tiles arranged in intricate patterns.

"I am afraid you will need to share a room."

"That's fine," Sarah said.

Grayle had never shared a room with a girl before. *How will I get changed? What if I snore? Do I smell?* He pretended to rub his cheek on his shoulder, casually sniffing his armpit. Two and a half days without a shower.

Not good.

Nazan opened the door to an almost empty room. Two thin mattresses were placed on the floor on opposite sides. The afternoon sun streamed through two doors opening onto a grand balcony. Sirens echoed from the direction of the Hagia Sophia. Emergency response teams.

Grayle hoped no one had gotten seriously hurt. Except for Mussels. He didn't mind if Mussels got injured. And Caine for that matter. *And* those four thugs who attacked him.

Nazan headed out of the room. "I will leave you to rest. We will prepare a meal. I will return for you then."

"Thanks," Grayle said.

Sarah kept quiet, her attention focused on the closing door.

"What's wrong?" he asked.

There'd been a tighter pinch to Sarah's face ever since their run-in with Caine.

Confronting your mother's killer will do that, Grayle figured.

"Nazan," Sarah said. "She's not being honest."

"What makes you say that?"

She tapped the soft skin beneath her eye. "Her aura keeps shifting hues. It darkened when she said she'd return—a sign when someone's being deceptive."

"But why help us escape only to deceive us later?" Like her, Grayle had a gut feeling Nazan didn't save them out of the goodness of her heart. But why the deceive them? What purpose could it serve?

"She could want something from us," Sarah suggested. "No one does anything without expecting something in return."

Grayle couldn't argue there. His last foster parents, Sly and Irma Zito, dangled news of his mysterious past like a carrot on a stick. They forced him to commit burglaries in exchange for the information—information that, in the end, they never had.

"Speaking of being deceptive, what's with the fake names? *Alistair*…really? The most popular and good-looking jock at Bayview Secondary? He's like the total opposite of me." Grayle grinned. "Except for the good-looking part."

Sarah rolled her eyes. "Don't flatter yourself. Those were just the first names that came to mind. The less anyone knows about us, the better"

"Why? You think Nazan suspects I'm a Hexhunter?"

She shrugged. "I don't know."

"Or that we're after the Eye of Odin?"

"I *don't* know."

"What about the runestone? You think Nazan can help us find it?"

"Grayle. I. Don't. Know." She exhaled and rubbed her forehead. "Look, I need to get some rest. I'll be able to think more clearly once I've recharged a bit. You should do the same."

Grayle did feel worn out, but sleep invited nightmares. He wasn't ready for one of those—not that he ever was. "You go ahead," he said.

Sarah chose the mattress farthest from the balcony. She adjusted her pillow and snuggled beneath a thin sheet already.

Grayle sat on the other mattress across from her. For the first time that day, he let his adrenaline fade. Exhaustion crept in; every part of him suddenly worn out.

At least we have a moment to catch our breaths, Grayle thought. *No one knows we're here.*

He laid back and slowly shut his eyes, drifting off into a deep sleep.

Chapter 19

The Operative stared at his phone's display. The tracking beacon stopped transmitting. He waited another few seconds, hoping it would return.

It didn't.

The red pulse overlaid on Google Maps had winked out completely.

They've crossed into Folklore, he guessed.

He localized where the signal disappeared and headed in that direction, moving through the streets, blending seamlessly into his surroundings like a chameleon. No one pestered him or paid him much attention; even shopkeepers left him in peace as he passed through the bazaar's winding corridors.

He'd discarded his security guard uniform and facial prosthetics soon after helping the Hexhunter escape.

What was I thinking, saving the witch and exposing myself so openly?

He feared he may have compromised his surveillance, maybe even the mission. He wasn't in the habit of saving lives—maybe once, a long time ago, in a different life. But he was an assassin now, a killer—whatever his employers needed him to be.

He scratched the scar tissue where his ears should have been. They were sliced off years earlier by Somali pirates during a botched covert operation. After his eventual rescue, the Operative returned the favor, finding each of the pirates in turn and cutting off *their* ears. He was dishonorably discharged from the Marine Corps soon after.

He didn't like to dwell on the past. But it was difficult not to, especially every time he looked in a mirror.

The Operative neared the location where the signal disappeared. He slowed and scanned ahead. According to his readings, the entrance to a Folklore was somewhere at the far end of the bustling south market. There was no indication a boundary or magical force field existed.

The Operative switched from his tracking app to the Inquisition's magic detection app. He aimed the phone's camera at a nondescript archway thirty feet down the passageway. The screen revealed a reddish haze fluctuating between the arch's supports like ripples in a pond.

As he suspected—a doorway into Folklore.

He knew the barriers protecting the Kingdoms of Folklore were practically impenetrable, hidden from Outlanders by invisibility incantations and clever teleportation spells. A trespasser would be transported across the Folklore without knowing what had happened. Legends spoke of only one person able to penetrate the magic: a Hexhunter. But they were killed off, most right at birth. Any who managed to slip through the cracks were hunted down by Folklore agents and murdered before reaching boyhood.

Except for this Grayle Rowen. He'd been able to survive.

The phone vibrated in his hand. The Operative looked down. Incoming call.

He switched from his detection app to the phone's keypad and answered.

"Report," demanded a man's voice.

German, the Operative surmised by the speaker's throaty R.

"I was forced to engage," he said.

"We are aware. Cleaners have been dispatched."

Cleaners—Inquisition crews who sterilized traces of Folklorian and Inquisition activity before Outlander authorities had a chance to investigate. Their work helped keep the existence of Folklore and the Inquisition a secret.

"Did the witch or Hexhunter see you?" the voice asked.

The Operative recalled the eye contact he and Rowen shared. Did he recognize him as his old substitute teacher? *Not likely—not with the prosthetics and costume disguising my features.*

Still, there was that moment.

"No, sir," he lied.

Pause.

"*Sehr Gut.* How will you proceed?"

"They've entered Folklore. I will continue tracking them once they re-emerge."

Another pause.

"Acceptable. However, you will not actively engage the targets again."

"Even if their lives are threatened?"

"That is correct."

That would make things difficult.

"Is there a problem with your orders, Operative?"

"I fail to see what use I'll be if I'm merely an observer."

"You will be doing the Inquisition's bidding. You must trust our judgment."

The Operative clenched his teeth. The last time he trusted his superiors, he ended up mutilated.

"Are you able to carry out the objectives of your mission?" the voice asked.

"Yes, sir."

"Good. Then keep us informed if anything changes."

As usual, the line went dead before the Operative could respond. Members of the Inner Circle weren't big on small talk. He respected that. More efficient and dispassionate that way.

He returned the phone to his jacket pocket.

A brusque wind swirled around him, kicking up dust and litter. Istanbul in March. The night would be cold. He had to find a place to hunker down.

The Operative climbed a fire escape to the roof of the nearest tenement building. He found a concealed vantage point from which he had a bird's eye view of the entire area. He sat against an exhaust vent, letting the warmth penetrate his shirt.

He thought back to his phone conversation. How were Cleaners dispatched to the Hagia Sophia so quickly? To have that kind of response time, there had to be other Inquisition agents on surveillance throughout the city.

He scratched at his scars.

Is the Inner Circle watching me?

Tracking the tracker—exactly the kind of paranoid strategy his employers would use.

Have I lost their confidence?

No matter. He couldn't let thoughts like that distract him. It didn't change the objective of his mission. And until his targets re-emerged, his mission was on stand-by.

Nothing to do now but wait.

Chapter 20

Sarah stood half-hidden in the balcony's doorway, gazing out over Istanbul's skyline in the late evening sunset. The balcony faced south, and across the rooftops she could see the minarets of the Blue Mosque and the shimmering Sea of Marmara. She heard kids laughing, music being played, and the constant buzz from the nearby Grand Bazaar.

But these weren't the sounds that had woken her. The aura had—the same one she'd sensed shortly before entering the Ottoman Folklore.

She had felt this distinct aura before. Just a little over a week ago, to be exact, when a squad of Crusaders had her trapped inside Bayview Secondary. She was in the process of hacking into the school's database to learn more about Grayle's mysterious past when a hit squad surrounded her.

Sarah's skin crawled at the memory.

She'd barely escaped with her life that night, almost killing some of the Crossers in the process. She knew full well that using magic to murder distorted her connection with the energy that gave a witch her power. Distort the connection enough times and a witch turned into a Hex. But in that kill or be killed situation, it was a price Sarah was willing to pay.

All to find out more about Grayle.

She turned. The boy was snoring when she'd woken up. He stirred restlessly on his mattress. Caught in another one of his nightmares?

What does a Hexhunter dream about? she wondered, forgetting for a moment that maybe he was a regular fifteen-year-old, that maybe he dreamed about what every other normal boy his age would.

Her cell phone went off.

Sarah looked at the display. A text message from Grigsby.

U ok? Where r u?

She bit her lip. Answering meant possibly giving away her location to anyone who was searching for her. But not answering would worry Grigs. The result could be the elf doing something stupid.

She wrote back: *Im ok. Will get back 2 u later.*

She never had the chance to tell him about Brenna's phone call or the warrant out for her arrest. As her Caretaker, he would be held partially responsible for her actions.

Grayle yawned, sat up and rubbed the heels of his palms into his eyes.

I also need to tell him about the bounty on his head.

She held back though, feeling guilty doing so. It was her selfish curiosity that had exposed Grayle to Folklore. Soon everyone would be aware of his existence. And then what?

He caught her staring.

"What is it?" he asked, his voice groggy.

Sarah held a finger to her lips. "Somebody's out there."

He got up and crossed to where she stood. "Yeah, like millions of Istanbullians."

He wasn't far from the truth. Pinpointing the aura was like trying to pick out a single voice in a crowded room—a *very* crowded room.

"It's someone specific," she said. "Step back for a second."

Sarah closed her eyes and swept her senses outward. Like shards of glass, a thousand emotions pierced her brain. *There.* Her mind brushed the familiar consciousness eighty yards away, lingering on a faraway rooftop. The aura felt cold, dangerous—as it did the night when the assassin it belonged to tried to kill her.

A shiver ran up Sarah's spine. She could feel the assassin's attention directed back at her. "He knows we're here. He's watching."

"Who? Who's out there?" Grayle asked, coming toward her again. His presence blanketed her senses like a cool wave, relieving her of the emotional flood.

"Not sure," she said, even though she was almost positive it belonged to the horribly scarred man with no ears.

Doubt crossed Grayle's face.

What…doesn't he believe me?

His reaction hurt.

"Did you get the runestone?" he asked, changing the subject.

In all the excitement, Sarah had forgotten about the stone she pulled from the Hagia Sophia's dome.

"Not exactly," she said.

Grayle's eyebrows dropped into a V.

Sarah dug into her pants pocket, producing the pebble-sized stone. She sat down and placed it on the floor.

"Ga'la," she whispered.

A blue glow flashed from her hand. The granite, and the tiny runes inscribed on it, grew ten times in size.

"That doesn't look like it belongs to the same runestone we found in Vancouver," Grayle said, taking a seat next to her.

"I know. But it's location in the dome couldn't have been a coincidence. We followed Halfdan's clues, and they were pretty specific. Whoever was searching for the runestone was supposed to find this. I'm sure of it."

Grayle nodded. "So what do the runes say?"

Sarah took out her laptop and opened the Folklore translator program. She entered the runes into the computer, double-checking to make sure she'd typed them in proper order, then clicked "Translate".

The deciphered text scrolled across the screen:

> *"Need you must the emeralds three,*
> *To use as the doorway's key,*
> *A mix of green stone and liquid red,*
> *To enter the tomb of those long dead.*
> *Heed the warnings on the wall,*
> *And avoid the traps that will kill you all."*

"Any clue what it means?" Grayle asked.

Sarah shook her head. "No idea. You mind?" She took his hand and placed it on the stone.

No additional runes glowed from its rugged surface.

"I guess that's it," Grayle said, sounding disappointed.

Sarah wasn't convinced. "Not necessarily."

"You found something?"

"It's more of what I'm *not* finding. There's no reference to another city, no new 'Capital of the East'—just a tomb. The lack of information makes me think the tomb is still in the city somewhere."

"It can be in a million different places though," Grayle said. "Unless there's someone around who can help us find it?"

"Unlikely. The last Varangians died two centuries ago. It's hard to say whether anyone living knows where this tomb might—"

Knock. Knock.

Sarah reached for her bedsheet and tossed it over the stone. "Yes?"

The door opened, and Nazan poked her head in. "Good, you're awake. There is a meeting upstairs. We have food and refreshments. We would like you to join us."

Was this an invitation, an order—or a trap?

"We'll be right there," Sarah said.

Grayle waited until the door clicked shut. "I have a bad feeling about this," he said.

Sarah shared his apprehension. If the Ottomans discovered they were after the Eye of Odin, if they discovered who Grayle really was, if they knew there was a price on his head and a warrant out for her, their situation could go from bad to worse.

She glimpsed beyond the balcony.

Then a Crosser assassin would be the least of our worries.

Chapter 21

"Don't say anything that might get us in trouble," Sarah warned.

They had left their room ten minutes after Nazan summoned them, walking along the open breezeway to the top floor.

Grayle gave her an exaggerated eye-roll. He wasn't a fan of pep talks or being lectured to—even when it came from her.

"Seriously," she said. "Our hunt for the Eye of Odin is a secret. It *has* to stay that way."

"Why would I say anything? I don't want anyone else to find the Eye either. Why don't we just get out of here? Keep searching for the runestone on our own?"

Sarah shook her head. "Not with those Crusaders still out there. For the time being, we're safer in here."

"You sure about that?"

Nazan appeared from a doorway ahead. Free of her headscarf, a mass of tight black curls ran wild from her head. "There you are. Everyone has arrived." She motioned for them to come in.

"Who's everyone?" Grayle whispered.

Sarah shrugged. "I think we're about to find out."

They entered a long, rectangular room, richly decorated with colorful ceramic tile. Floor to ceiling windows scattered the sunset's orange and pink hues across the marble floor. Four men, ranging in age from their late thirties to early fifties, lounged on a rug in the middle of the room. They smoked tobacco from a hookah, a lamp-like, glass vase with a long tube snaking from its base. A bluish haze hung above their heads.

Nazan made introductions. "This is Butrus and his brother, Hamza. My cousin, Yusuf. And this is Abbas Bekir." She gestured to the oldest of them perched on several red and purple cushions. He had a curled, white mustache and plump, ruddy cheeks that reminded Grayle of a beardless Santa Claus. "These are the visitors from the Norse Folklore I told you about: Brenna and Alistair."

Sarah gave a short bow. Grayle awkwardly did the same, distracted by brass bowls filled with food arranged on the carpet.

"You've come a long way," said the mustached Abbas. He gestured for them to sit and join them on the carpet.

The rug's wool fabric felt soft as they sat.

One of the men, Hamza, sank into a pillow and smiled broadly, revealing nicotine-stained teeth. He offered Grayle the hose from the hookah. Grayle raised a hand and shook his head. He didn't smoke and wasn't about to start now. The steaming dishes laid out before him, however, were more enticing.

It had been a long day, and food was exactly what he needed. There were meatballs, roasted lamb, a flat bread topped with meat, and what looked like a syrupy, pastry dessert sprinkled with ground pistachios. He reached hungrily for something that looked like a canoe-shaped pizza when Sarah grabbed his wrist. She shook her head and, without saying a word, stuck her chin out at Abbas Bekir, sitting regally on his pillows.

The older man closed his eyes and recited a small prayer: "Bismillahi wa barakatillah."

When he opened them again, he gestured toward the food.

Grayle looked to Sarah for permission.

She nodded.

He picked up the pizza and bit into it.

"Brenna and Alistair were in the Hagia Sophia during the earthquake today," Nazan informed the others. "They were being attacked, and I offered them safe haven."

The way she spoke sounded rehearsed. Grayle figured Nazan had told these men exactly what she'd seen after bringing him and Sarah to their guest room. So why the act?

"Who attacked you?" asked the one Nazan introduced as Butrus. He had black, thinning hair that stuck to his scalp in a bad combover. He stared at them with dark, suspicious eyes.

"That's our business," Grayle said through a mouthful of food.

Sarah elbowed him in the ribs. "Sorry. Alistair is still a little shaken after our ordeal. We believe whoever attacked us had mistaken us for someone else. They could've been Crossers, we're not sure. Either way, we need safe passage back to our ship. Would you be willing to help us?"

"If it's a simple case of safe passage you require, perhaps we can help each other." Abbas reached behind him and produced a large scroll. He unrolled the parchment on the rug, revealing blueprints for a large building complex.

"What's this?" Sarah asked.

"This is the interior of the Topkapi Palace," Abbas explained. "It used to be the focal point of our Folklore for almost six hundred years."

"It also houses some of the Ottoman Folklore's most priceless relics," Butrus added.

"And you're showing us this...why?" Grayle asked. His internal "caution" alarm was going off.

"We want our relics back," Abbas replied curtly.

Grayle stopped chewing and traded a suspicious glance with Sarah. Here it was, the real reason they were brought to the Ottoman Folklore.

Sarah's expression remained stone-faced. "What makes you think we can help?"

"You are a witch," Nazan said matter-of-factly. "Do not try to deny it," she added, quickly lifting a hand to stop Sarah from protesting. "Not only were you the targets of Crusaders today, but you had the undead after you as well—which means you are in trouble with some powerful gods." She paused, waiting for Sarah to admit the truth. "Now that is who you are, but I am not entirely sure about him." She nodded toward Grayle. "He is too young to be your Caretaker and does not appear to be a warlock. Boyfriend, maybe?"

"He is," Sarah answered.

Grayle threw her a startled look. She gave him an imperceptible nod that meant *Go with me on this.*

"Let's say for a minute I am who you think I am," Sarah continued. "What would you need a witch to retrieve for you?"

"Three artifacts," Abbas answered. "The Holy Banner, the Spoonmaker's Diamond, and the Emerald Dagger."

Grayle edged closer to the map. "Spoonmaker. Strange name for a diamond."

"Yes, but appropriate," Yusuf conceded. Next to Nazan, he was the youngest of the Ottomans gathered in the room and shared the same almond-shaped eyes as his cousin. "It is said that a fisherman found the diamond on a rubbish heap. He brought it to market, where a jeweler told him it was a worthless piece of glass and that he would give the fisherman three spoons for his trouble. The fisherman accepted, not knowing he was handing over an immense treasure—the fourth largest diamond in the world. For this reason, the gemstone became known as the Spoonmaker's Diamond."

"We also know exactly where the relics are located. They are situated in different exhibits here, here and here." Butrus pointed to three separate locations on the map.

Grayle leaned in. "Do you have a layout of the exhibit interiors?"

"Sadly, no. Photographs are strictly forbidden inside the palace."

"That's a problem," Grayle said, studying the designs.

"There is an even greater problem. The Romans control the Palace and all the treasures within."

"But I thought owning another Folklore's relics is forbidden," Sarah pointed out.

Grayle knew she was playing dumb.

"Correct," Butrus said. "But the Romans believe the land, people, and all the relics in their previously occupied territories belong to them."

"Why would they want artifacts from other Folklores?" Grayle asked, crunching into one of the syrupy pastries. Suspicious or not, he wasn't going to let the food go to waste.

"Power," Abbas said simply. His jolly demeanor suddenly turned serious. "The old peace that has sustained our realms for hundreds of years is disintegrating. There is talk of the Inquisition killing witches again, kidnapping soothsayers, systematically undermining relations between Folklores. Kingdoms are turning on each other, forging alliances to intimidate less powerful kingdoms, and taking their artifacts to secure their power."

Grayle studied the drawings on the blueprint, only half-listening to Abbas' explanation. He was nagged by something on the map. He shifted on the carpet, trying to get a better look. The sketch was plainly crude, with cryptic notations written in Arabic along the sides and bottom. But as he examined it closer, he realized what was troubling him. A symbol—tucked away in the right-hand corner. A circle with a cross in the center.

Grayle almost choked on his pastry.

It was the Odin Cross.

Chapter 22

Butterflies fluttered in Sarah's stomach. Like Grayle, she recognized the circled cross on the palace blueprints. She met his gaze, the question plain in his eyes: *What was the mark of Odin doing on an ancient Ottoman map?*

It was the same question Sarah wanted answered, and the very question she couldn't ask.

"What kind of security are we looking at?" Grayle asked. "In the palace, I mean."

Hamza spoke for the first time, his voice high and nasally. "The Romans have Outlander clothed security at all entrances and exits." He pointed to three gates inside the Topkapi complex. Each one led into another walled-in courtyard.

"What about the artifacts themselves?"

"The Spoonmaker's Diamond is kept under high security here, in the Imperial Treasury." Yusuf tapped one of the buildings in the innermost courtyard. "Round the clock guards, pressure plates, laser sensors, and cameras protect it."

"It will fetch a mighty sum on the black market," Hamza said greedily. Then, noticing Abbas's disapproving glare, added, "If we

111

decide to sell it, of course."

Yusuf cleared his throat. "The second artifact is the Holy Banner. It belonged to the prophet Muhammad, peace be upon him, and was carried into battle by many of our armies in the past. It became the standard that rallied our troops. It is said whoever carries the Banner into battle would emerge victorious."

"We will need it for the struggle ahead," Butrus said grimly.

"So do others," said Yusuf. "Rumor has it the Persians are trying to acquire the Banner from the Romans."

"Why would they want it?" asked Grayle.

Yusuf shrugged. "To help them on some venture. They are also negotiating an arms deal—their loyalty in exchange for Roman weapons and ships."

"And what about the Emerald Dagger?" Sarah interrupted. She wanted to keep the conversation on topic.

"Little is known about the dagger. It was believed to have come from South America, but its true origins are in dispute. Some say it was a gift from the gods, some believe it came from the Varangians—used in murder plots and assassinations."

Sarah perked at the mention of Varangians.

"The dagger is also in the Imperial Treasury," Yusuf continued, "protected by alarms, a tempered glass casing, and surrounded by pressure plates."

"Do you have pictures of the artifacts?" Sarah asked.

Nazan handed her an iPad.

Sarah scrolled through each image, stopping at the dagger. It couldn't have been more than a foot long. The blade itself was hidden in a diamond-encrusted scabbard. The intricate relief of a flower bouquet adorned the center. As tantalizing as the gold and diamonds were, Sarah's eyes were drawn to the dagger's hilt. Three green emeralds, the size of golf balls, sat fastened into the handle.

Need you must the emeralds three,
To use as the doorway's key,

Sarah swallowed. *The emeralds three.*

Bingo.

The inscription on the clue stone was beginning to make sense.

"What magic levels are we talking about?" she asked, trying to keep her cool. She passed the iPad to Grayle. He recognized the dagger's importance right away.

"The diamond possesses no magic. Both the banner and dagger are registered as Level 1 artifacts."

"But you must understand," Yusuf added, "the worth of these artifacts does not only reside in their magical power, but in their ability to inspire our Folklore to rise up against the Romans. The Holy Banner itself will rally our people. The dagger and diamond will fund our campaign and help feed our people. For a short time, at least."

"We've been under the Roman heel for too long," said Butrus. "They have all the advantages, all the weaponry, all the manpower, all the money. Even as we speak, our leaders are attempting to broker a deal with the local Roman governor."

"Um, stealing artifacts during negotiations can't be good for diplomacy," Grayle said.

Sarah agreed. "If the Romans find out what you're planning, the negotiations will end…and none too friendly either. Unless that's what you want."

Their silence confirmed her suspicion.

She exhaled. "The Ottoman leadership doesn't know what you're up to, do they?"

"They do not," Butrus admitted. "Any deals our leaders achieve will be one-sided. But if the people learn that we have been able to retrieve three of our most sacred artifacts from under watchful Roman eyes—"

"It could give us some leverage at the negotiation table," Nazan cut in. "Let the Romans know we're not as weak as they think we are."

Sarah shook her head. "This could end badly. The Romans could just as easily come in force and take what they want."

"These are risks we are willing to take."

Grayle leaned forward. "Yeah, but why should *we* risk *our* necks for you? Why don't you just steal the relics yourself?"

Butrus took a long drag from the Hookah, then expelled the smoke through his nose. "Our Folklore has no Loremaster, no witches, no magickers of any kind. We are left with good, hard-working common folk, but no one with the skills we require. Not even our agents have been able to get close enough to the artifacts. It is well to assume the Romans have information about many of us, maybe even complete dossiers. Our younger agents, like Nazan and those foreign to our land, may be more unexpected."

"And that is why we need you," Abbas pointed out.

Everyone on the carpet went silent again, their eyes fixed on Sarah.

She saw the desperation in their faces. Her Auralex senses touched their pain, anger, despair and the sacrifices they had to endure under Roman rule. Now they wanted an answer.

Sarah wasn't sure what to tell them.

She came to Istanbul to find another piece of Mimir's Stone, not to get sidetracked by a different mission. In a way, finding the Eye and keeping it from those who could destroy the world was helping the Ottomans, wasn't it? After all, this was their world too.

Ugh. Where's Grigsby when I need him?

She relied on his guidance when it came to missions like this. Despite the danger, she knew what he'd say: "Relievin' artifacts from people they don't belong to is your mandate as a witch-for-hire, Sarah."

And he'd be right.

"We'll need to talk this over in private. Can we have a moment?" she asked.

Abbas gave her an impatient smile. "Of course."

Sarah motioned for Grayle to follow her. They moved to a plush, velvet couch in the farthest alcove of the room. They sat, purposely turning their backs to their hosts so as not to be overheard.

"What do you think?" Grayle asked.

"They're still not telling us the whole truth," she said. "But whatever their agenda might be, we need that dagger. The runestone marker is somewhere in the city—the Odin Cross on the map confirms that much."

Grayle was slow to nod. "I know…that can't be a coincidence. But stealing *three* artifacts from a fortified palace, a palace with three walls…not to mention guards and state-of-the-art security systems! We were almost killed trying to take just one artifact from a Canadian museum—small potatoes in comparison to what we're planning here."

"Are you saying we can't do it?" Sarah didn't mean for it to sound like a dare, but that's how it came out.

Grayle squinted and drew his brows together. "I'm saying it'll be risky is all, especially with Caine, Mussels, and Crusaders looking for us."

And a price on our heads, Sarah reminded herself, a fact she wasn't about to reveal right then.

"This is our only lead," she said. "If we don't figure out what the symbol on the map represents, our search for the Eye ends here."

Grayle ran his fingers through his hair. "So we'll need to kill two birds with one stone—help the Ottomans retrieve their artifacts and figure out what the Odin symbol clue means…maybe even find the runestone—"

"An' then get outta the city faster than a jackrabbit in front of a prairie fire," Sarah added, doing her best Grigsby impersonation.

They both smiled, relieving some of the tension about what they were planning to do.

"I'm going to need to scope out the palace and exhibits beforehand though," Grayle said. "There's no way I'm going in there blind."

Sarah nodded and let out a long breath. "It's settled then."

They walked back to where Nazan, Abbas, and the others waited.

"We'll do it," Sarah said. "We'll help you retrieve your artifacts."

Chapter 23

The spirit looked tiny standing in vastness of the grand hall. She blended with the surrounding gray stone and shadows. Her plain, filthy gown was marred by a bloodstain—a constant reminder of the bullet that ended her life.

Skoll and Manegarm paced around the spectre like two sharks circling a lone seal. A ring of burning embers trailed in their wake, confining the ghost behind a smoky barrier.

The spirit either ignored or was unaware of the Hel-hounds' presence. She stood motionless, her head low, shoulders slumped, her skin as white as...well, a ghost.

Hel was accustomed to the crushed spirits roaming her kingdom. Once cast into Helheim for an eternity of torment, the dead quickly lost all hope. Not that they had anything to live for.

Rachel Finn was no different.

When she first arrived, the former witch had insisted she didn't belong in Helheim, arguing that her accomplishments in life deserved a one-way ticket to Valhalla—Odin's hall of heroes. Finn was in no position to bargain, however. Hel's power not only derived from the amount of souls she reaped, but from the strength the souls possessed in life. Rachel Finn had been powerful when she was alive. Hel was lucky to have her.

Even luckier now.

"Rachel Finn." Hel's voice boomed in the hush of the hall. "You have been summoned for a special purpose."

The spirit lifted her head. Hollow eyes blinked through a curtain of straight, black hair. "What purpose is that, your grace?" Finn's words sounded distant, as if she were speaking from another plane of existence. In a way, she was.

Hel leaned forward on her throne. The motion sent a jolt of pain radiating through her body. She suppressed the discomfort. "A purpose that will see you reunited with your daughter."

The spirit stood straighter. "M-my daughter?" She brushed the hair from her face. Despite the hollow eyes and ashen texture to her skin, Rachel Finn was stunning.

Her beauty angered Hel. It only served as a reminder of how ugly she was in comparison.

"Yes, anything." Finn stepped closer. "Tell me what I must do."

Skoll and Manegarm snarled at her sudden movement.

The spectre froze, not daring to come closer.

Hel rested her elbows on the armrests and laced her fingers. "I am pleased you are so eager to help," she said.

The spirit's expression switched from hope to wary suspicion. "What must I do, your grace?"

"It appears as though your daughter is following in your footsteps. She is on the hunt for the Eye of Odin, accompanied by the only surviving Hexhunter known to exist. She must be desperate if she is allying herself with a mortal enemy."

The spirit covered her mouth and took a step backward. "You must do something, your grace," she said with a touch of horror. "You cannot allow her to—"

Hel shot to her feet. More pain spasmed. "Do not presume to tell me what I must do—especially in my own hall!" Her voice carried across the chamber, causing the walls to shudder.

Finn's spirit dropped to her knees. Her gaze found the floor.

That's more like it. The picture of supplication.

Hel smiled and sat as the rumbling settled. "As I was saying," she continued more softly, "your daughter is in league with a Hexhunter. I assume you realize the implications of their partnership?"

The spirit remained on her knees. Her head nodded slowly.

"Good. Whatever may happen in the coming weeks, I need your daughter on *my* side."

"Your side, my Queen?"

"Yes. I need you to convince her to find the remaining runestones—and then hand them over to *me*."

Hel regretted not thinking of this plan earlier. She could have saved herself the unpleasantness of having to retrieve the runestones, the humiliation of seeking out Sebastian Caine's help, and of having to reveal herself and risking the interference of the other gods. *They must know what I'm up to by now,* she thought. *But if the witchling could be persuaded to do the retrieving for me, then I'd be able to—*

"No," the spirit's voice squeaked.

Hel paused, unsure whether she heard the spectre correctly. "No?"

Rachel Finn shook her head and got to her feet. "Do you take me for a fool?" she said, her posture suddenly defiant, rebellious. Skoll and Manegarm growled, warning her to respect their mistress. She ignored them. "I will never coerce my daughter to do your bidding," the ghost continued. "There's nothing you can do that will make me put her in harm's way."

"Nothing I can do?" Hel thrust out an arm. Ropes of black magic spiralled from her fingers. Like jungle vines, they tangled around the spirit's neck. "Nothing. *I*. Can. Do?" She rose from her seat.

The spirit gagged, trying in vain to pull the tendrils from her throat.

"There is so much I can do," Hel threatened. "I am the goddess of death. What makes you think I cannot impose my will upon the dead *and* the living? If you do not do as I ask," Hel hissed, "it is your daughter who will feel my wrath. Would you rather she enjoys my hospitality here in Helheim? Or perhaps I can have her join Thrain's legion of walking dead?"

Finn shook her head. "Even if…I ask her…to do as you wish—" the spirit rasped beneath Hel's stranglehold, "Sarah will…never help you."

The goddess smiled. "Then for her sake, and yours, I hope you're good at changing minds. I wager a daughter's love can be persuaded to do almost anything, especially if visited by her long dead mother."

"You'd allow me to see her?"

"For a short time…yes. But only if you do as I ask."

Hel released her magic, and Finn fell to the floor. "If she is successful in doing what I ask, I will grant your daughter a wish the both of you cannot refuse. Now listen carefully. This is what I am willing to do…"

Chapter 24

Grayle stood on a raised platform in a room dimly lit with torches. He held a broadsword in his little hands, using much of his strength to simply lift the weapon. Even though he knew this was a dream, he felt the jitters in his stomach. But this wasn't like the dreams he had before. Those felt like nightmares, while this seemed…different.

"Again," commanded the woman in the feathered cloak.

No sooner had Grayle positioned himself in a ready stance when a different woman, dressed in a fitted metal breastplate and leather arm guards, rushed forward. She swung a double-bladed axe at his head.

Grayle ducked, sidestepped, then lashed out wildly. He missed, and the weight of his sword threw him off balance.

Using the axe handle, the woman jabbed Grayle between his shoulder blades. He cried out, the impact forcing him on all fours.

"Again," said the woman in the feathered cloak.

"Forget it!" Grayle shouted. His voice sounded young, high pitched. "I don't want to do this anymore."

Hands on her hips, the woman's deep brown eyes fixed on his. "You do not have a choice."

"Why? Why are you making me do this?"

"For good reasons."

"Then tell me."

"Now is not the time." She stood taller and readjusted her cloak. "Again."

"I won't, not until you—"

"Again!" her voice boomed. The surrounding torches blazed brighter.

Grayle cursed under his breath. Using the sword as a crutch, he pushed himself back on his feet.

The woman with the axe stared at him. Swan feathers attached to her shoulder plates looked like wings. But she was no angel—Grayle was certain of it. Her eyes were hard, focused on her next plan of attack. The sinewy muscles in her arms flexed as she prepared herself.

He lifted his sword for the umpteenth time, and the woman lunged.

Grayle tried to block her swing. She was stronger, knocking the sword from his grip. It clattered out of reach. Defenceless, Grayle couldn't react fast enough. The woman strafed her elbow across his jaw, sending him sprawling onto the wooden platform.

Grayle tasted blood. The room moved dizzily around him.

"Finish it, Sigrun," said the woman in the feathered cloak. "Maybe then he will learn his lesson."

The axe came swooping down, the butt end rushing toward Grayle's face.

White light exploded behind his eyes.

He bolted upright, gasping.

It was dark, except for the moonlight streaming through the open balcony doors. All was quiet in the guest room.

Grayle forced his body to relax. Just once he wished for normal dreams, full of pleasant thoughts, maybe with unicorns or dancing hippos. Maybe dreams about his parents, was that too much to ask? Instead, his nightmares were getting worse—and more confusing. This dream had been much different from the ones before. Gone were the woods. The cold. The darkness. In a previous dream, the woman in the black feathered cloak had saved him from a zombie herd.

She wasn't saving me this time.

Grayle reached for his temple, expecting to feel a lump where the axe handle had struck him. Nothing. But it had felt so real.

It seemed like I was being trained for something, but why—and for what?

Lost in thought, Grayle never noticed the dark shadow standing in the corner until it moved into the moonglow. His heart leapt to his throat. At first, he thought it was the assassin Sarah had sensed earlier, but, spotting crows perched on each shoulder, the intruder's identity became clear.

Odin.

A black patch covered his right eye, and his long beard, tied into four braids, gleamed white in the moonlight.

"What are you doing here?" Grayle whispered, glancing at Sarah at the far side of the room. Her blanket gently rose and fell in time with her breathing.

"Forgive me for startling you, Hexhunter. But I have urgent news."

"It couldn't wait until morning? And thanks, by the way, for not telling me I'm a Hexhunter when you had the chance. You could've saved me a lot of grief."

"Some things need to be experienced rather than told, lad."

"What the hell does that mean?"

"You will know in time."

One of the crows on the All-Father's shoulders stuck its beak in his ear.

"Yes, yes...the urgent news," Odin said, then turned back to Grayle. "Fortune has brought you closer to the next runestone, lad. All you need now is the key."

Grayle rubbed his forehead in frustration. "Key? You wanna fill me in on what you're talking about?"

"You were correct in assuming the Emerald Dagger is the key to opening the Tomb of Serpents. You will need to steal it if you are to be successful."

Grayle sat up straighter. *Tomb of Serpents?* Was he talking about *the tomb of those long dead* mentioned on the clue stone? Or *the serpent's doorway* mentioned in the Viking runes etched in the Hagia Sophia? Regardless, Grayle didn't like the sound of serpents. Snakes made him squeamish. "And if we do steal it, then what? Where's this Tomb?"

Odin opened his mouth to answer, then hesitated.

"What? Don't you know where it is?" Grayle asked, stunned that the god would tell him to go somewhere and not know how to get there.

"Huginn and Muninn will guide you to it," he answered.

The two birds flapped their wings proudly.

"*They're* going to show me?" Grayle asked, unconvinced.

The All-Father nodded. "They are my ears and—"

"Eyes in this vast world," Grayle interrupted. "Yeah, you told me that before. But if I'm going to do this, I'm going to need something in return this time."

The All-Father grimaced. "I am not in the habit of bargaining with mortals." His tone turned deep and menacing. "What is it you want?"

Grayle thought about telling him of the woman in the black feathered cloak. At the very least, the god could find out who she was. But something in the way Odin looked at him made

Grayle change his mind. "Nothing yet, but I'll let you know when I do."

"Very well," Odin said. "For now, steal the dagger and await Huginn and Muninn." He walked out onto the balcony. The silver moonlight washed over his misshapen hat and gray cloak. "And do not fail. The future of mankind depends on you." With that, the Norse god jumped off the balcony, disappearing into the night.

Grayle didn't bother to check if he'd gone splat on the cobblestones below. He was no longer fazed by gods, witches, or zombies—not even when they jumped off three storey buildings.

Sarah stirred from her sleep. "You say something?" she asked drowsily.

"No. Go to sleep."

She lay back on her side and resumed her gentle snoring.

How was he going to explain his visits with Odin to her? He said he was going to be honest.

Grayle flopped onto his mattress.

He stared at the ceiling. Questions instead of hippos danced in his head until the sun rose.

Chapter 25

Midgard, Norse Folklore

It was early morning when Brenna stepped onto Midgard's fortifications. The city stirred to life behind her. The smell of campfires from longhouse hearths drifted over rooftops. Merchants swept the wooden sidewalks in front of their stalls. Shepherds led their flocks to pasture.

Brenna loved this place. It had been the home of her father, and her father's father before him, all the way to Ragnar Lodbrok, her infamous Viking ancestor who raided England and Paris centuries ago. He was fearless, adventurous, and hot-headed—Brenna wondered if that's where she inherited *her* temper.

And now father's threatening to send me away from here. Not a chance.

As much as she loved her mother and yearned to be with her at times, Midgard was her home—the place she was meant to be.

She turned her gaze a mile down the waterway, where the enchanted mist hung over the fjord. It had kept Midgard's existence hidden from Outlanders for over a thousand years and was meant to protect her from the dangers that lurked outside its walls.

Not anymore.

None of the barriers, natural or magical, could protect her from enemies within.

As promised, Brenna had kept her warrior dress on all night. The stiff leather had dug into her hip, making sleep impossible. But wardrobe discomfort was only partially to blame for her insomnia. At any moment, she expected her bedroom door to burst open, for Hel's black robed outline to reach out, snare and whisk her away into the night again. There was no reason for Hel to return, Brenna knew that, but there remained the small matter of finding the traitor who let the goddess into Midgard. And after yesterday's meeting, it was clear finding the traitor would be left to her.

A black streak soared across the sky, distracting Brenna from her thoughts. It was a crow with ink stained wings, circling high above her.

Brenna put two fingers to her lips and whistled.

The bird dove, swooped in a wide arch, and landed atop her shoulder.

"Good morning, Hrafn. How are you?"

The crow blinked and cawed. *Hungry.*

"I thought you might be." She pulled a piece of dried pork from her pocket and fed it to the bird.

As a Dyr'talara, Brenna was able to process an animal's thoughts and language into words. Her skills were limited to translating only two words at a time. But as she grew older and her connection to her magic strengthened, Brenna hoped to increase that number. But for now, two words were enough.

"Who's a pretty bird?" Brenna cooed.

Hrafn looked to his left and right, then cawed. *I am.*

"That's right." She stroked his tarry feathers. "You are."

Hrafn had been her companion for the past three years, ever since she found him with an injured wing and nursed him back to health. He wasn't exactly her pet. He lived outside in the wild, but came when she called him. Bjorn complained about his pungent smell and threatened to cook him for dinner several times.

Human coming, Hrafn cawed.

The crow tilted his head, focused on a boy approaching from the top of Midgard's main gate. He wore armor two sizes too large. His shirt sleeves covered his hands, and his belt drooped well past his waist. It was Fell Halvarson, the Wall Guard's newest recruit and just the person Brenna wanted to see.

"We have some work to do today," she whispered to Hrafn. "I'll need your eyes in the sky, okay?"

The crow cawed his understanding and winged from her shoulder.

"*Hailsa*, Brenna. What brings a magicker to the ramparts this early?" Fell flashed her a brilliant smile. "I don't see Svein anywhere. Are you sure it's safe to be outside without your protector?"

"Shut up," Brenna grumbled. A protector was the last thing she needed, and Fell knew it.

They had been close friends for years, playing together and causing mischief since they were toddlers. Things changed as they grew older though. With Brenna gone for months on end for magicker training and Fell's appointment to the Wall Guard, they'd slowly grown apart. There was an untold barrier between them now—invisible, but it was there.

"You didn't kill Svein, did you?" Fell teased.

At least he hadn't lost his sense of humor.

Brenna shook her head. "I brewed an extra-strength laxative and slipped it into his morning mead. He'll be on the toilet all day—maybe tomorrow too."

Fell laughed. "Who knew your elixir classes would come in handy?"

Next to her incineration spells, elixir class had been one of Brenna's worst. Dyr'talaras weren't known for their magical talents beyond communicating with animals.

"But seriously, what *are* you doing here?" Fell asked.

"Loremaster Onem wants me to inspect the fortifications for weaknesses."

Fell puffed out his chest. "You'll find no weaknesses here," he said proudly.

"Not here, of course. But there has to be some sections that aren't being patrolled on a regular basis."

Something in Fell's reaction told her she was right.

"C'mon," she said. "Tell me what you know. For old time's sake. "

He laughed again. "For old time's sake? We're fourteen! We're too young to have *old times*." His eyes narrowed. "This has nothing to do with what happened to you, does it? The kidnapping?"

"It has *everything* to do with that!" The words came out harsher than Brenna wanted them to. "I need your help, Fell," she said, bringing her voice back to an even pitch. "Hel got into the city. If there's even the slightest chance a breach occurred, wouldn't you want to find out where and make sure it doesn't happen again?"

Fell's eye twitched, the way it used to when she beat him at *hnefatafl*, their favorite board game. He sighed and leaned in. "If such a thing did take place," he whispered, "which officially I'm not saying it did, it would have been done quickly, in a more isolated part of the wall. If it were me, I would have chosen the northern defenses, where the chasm of Idun Falls meets the Pillar of Halvor. Not even a Jotun could climb it, so it's often left unattended."

Brenna knew the place. It was remote but close enough to reach this afternoon.

"The magical incantations would have prevented anyone from getting in though, right?" Fell asked. It seemed like he was looking for reassurance.

"Right," Brenna said, doing her best to sound optimistic. "But Onem wants me to check…just to be sure."

Fell huffed. "Yeah. Sure he does."

He clearly didn't believe her. That was fine. The less Fell knew, the less he would be held responsible if she was caught snooping in places she didn't belong.

"Fell!" Einar Halvarson, Fell's father, came tromping up the ramparts. He had been Midgard's sentry captain for as long as Brenna could remember. "Get back to your post before I have you whipped." His armor gleamed in the morning sunlight, and a great plume of white horse hair trailed down the back of his helmet.

"I'll see you later," Fell called out. His oversized helmet wobbled as he ran back to his post. Einar kicked him in the rear as he passed by.

"Morgen, Captain," Brenna said.

"What are you doing here, magicker?" Einar asked. His tone and body language were tense. "You're not filling Fell's head with fantasy tales, are you? Goddesses coming to steal away children in the dead of night?"

"It's not a *tale*," Brenna countered defensively. "I *was* kidnapped by Hel."

Einar let out an unfriendly chuckle. "Perhaps you had a nightmare, or a hallucination, believing you—"

"I was kidnapped!" Brenna's voice carried to a group of soldiers huddled at the far end of the ramparts.

Stay calm. No need to make a scene.

The captain came closer, his movement accompanied by a waft of rawhide and adult sweat. "Now you listen to me, *magicker*. I don't know what you are planning, but I don't want you causing trouble where none exists. And I don't want you getting my son involved." He wagged a finger in Brenna's face. "Just so you know, anyone caught trespassing in places where they don't belong will be punished accordingly. Anyone," he repeated, "from the most powerful, to the most puny."

Puny.

It was the exact word Loremaster Onem used in yesterday's briefing. The old warlock questioned why Hel would kidnap a puny witch like her. He had stopped mid-sentence to say a *young* witch, but his slip revealed his true opinion of Brenna and her abilities. In his eyes, she was insignificant—a Dyr'talara—hardly worth consideration. Not even important enough to kidnap.

I'm not puny or insignificant. The traitor and everyone else will learn that soon enough.

"I appreciate your advice, Captain," Brenna said, trying her best to be gracious. It didn't come easy.

Einar grunted and returned to his post atop Midgard's gate.

Brenna tipped her head back, welcoming the crisp morning breeze to brush her face. The coolness did little to chill her temper or her resolve. Despite the captain's threat, she was going ahead with her plan: find the evidence, expose the traitor, and save the city.

Chapter 26

Grayle doubted there'd be enough water for a shower, especially after seeing the dried out fountain in the villa's courtyard yesterday. He was surprised when a cold stream sputtered from the nozzle. He turned in the tiny cubicle, letting the water soothe his aching muscles and the bruises left by his tangle with the Taser-toting Crusaders. He watched the water swirl down the drain. If only more problems could wash away so easily.

Grayle spent the early morning hours mulling over his conversation with Odin. The All-Father basically confirmed that he and Sarah were on the right track. They just needed the Emerald Dagger to get into this Tomb of Serpents—*wherever that was*—and retrieve their first runestone.

After Sarah had woken up, they hashed out a plan for the morning: case out the exhibits where the three Ottoman artifacts were stored and determine what kind of security they were dealing with. Grayle knew he'd have to channel his inner thief again. The thieving skills he'd learned during his stint at the Gloomshroud Camp for Delinquent Youth had proven useful on several occasions. They would do so again.

Stepping out of the shower, Grayle noticed his clothes were missing.

Is someone playing a trick on me?

Luckily there was a towel. He dried himself off and wrapped it tight around his waist.

Sarah was already dressed by the time he scuttled into their guest room. Her eyebrows lifted when she saw him standing there half-naked. She smiled. "That may not be the right outfit for where we're going today."

Grayle had no witty comeback. It was impossible to play things cool while only wearing a towel.

Sarah picked up on his discomfort. "Relax. Someone came by and left us fresh clothes." She pointed to a pair of cargo pants and a blue T-shirt folded on his mattress.

Crisis averted.

Grayle shuffled over and picked up the army green cargos. "Um, you mind turning around while I get dressed?"

Sarah's cheeks went red. "Oh, yeah. Sure. Sorry." She spun and faced the balcony.

Grayle put on the pants. They were a little loose around the waist but otherwise fit fine. Sarah had on a similar pair, only more form fitting. *How did she look that good without showering?* he wondered.

She stuck a hair tie in her mouth and pulled her hair into a ponytail.

"Don't tell me there's a spell for getting rid of morning bed-head," Grayle said.

"A girl can't reveal all her secrets," she answered.

He could tell she was smiling, even though he couldn't see her face. It was the playful tone in her voice.

"I updated Grigsby while you were in the shower."

"And? What did Mr. Sunshine have to say?"

"He's going to meet us outside the Topkapi Palace. He's not thrilled at including Nazan in our plans."

"Neither am I, but we may need her expertise." Grayle slid the T-shirt over his head. "And as the saying goes, *keep your friends close and your enemies closer.*"

There was a knock at the door.

"Come in."

Nazan entered, carrying more clothes. "Excellent. You're ready," she said.

"Almost." Grayle plopped on the mattress and slipped on his socks, a little embarrassed when his big toe popped out at the end.

Nazan handed Sarah a fine cloth made of cashmere wool. "It is customary for women to cover their heads when visiting the Topkapi Palace. They are strict about their dress codes—no shorts, tank tops…that sort of thing. This is a pashmina. Here, let me help you put it on."

Nazan draped the fine material over Sarah's head and shoulders. She folded the fabric under Sarah's chin and wrapped it again around her head. When she finished, the pashmina hid Sarah's hair, ears, and neck, leaving only her face exposed.

"Works as a disguise too," Sarah said, looking at her reflection in the balcony door's glass.

"I was thinking the same thing. I brought these for you as well." Nazan gave Grayle a Toronto Blue Jays baseball cap and a pair of sunglasses.

Grayle combed his fingers through his damp hair and gladly put them on. Even though he couldn't be seen by cameras, he could still be IDed with the naked eye. And another run-in with Mussels and the Crossers was the last thing he wanted.

"We best be going," Nazan said. "The Palace opens soon."

They exited the Ottoman Folklore through a different gate than the one they came in. Neither Abbas nor any of the other men from last night's meeting were there to see them off. Grayle didn't think much of it at the time.

They hurried along cobbled roads that clung to the brink of a cliff. The morning sun blazed in the western sky without a single cloud to keep it company. The Bosphorus Strait stretched before them all the way to the horizon, shimmering and sparkling in the sunlight.

Sarah fidgeted with the strap of her laptop bag, casting nervous glances over her shoulder.

"What is it?" Grayle asked.

She pursed her lips, a telltale sign something was wrong. "I can feel his aura. He's following us."

"The Crosser assassin?"

She nodded, looking behind her again.

Grayle had seen Sarah take on Hel, her Hel-hounds, and a posse of teenage girls back at school, but this Crusader seemed to disturb her most. "There's nothing we can do about him right now," he said. "As long as he's following us and not attacking us, we're gold."

Sarah didn't look convinced.

Grayle took her hand and gave it a reassuring squeeze. "For appearances," he said when she gave him a surprised look. "I am your boyfriend after all."

She smiled and seemed to relax a little. "Don't mention anything about the Crosser to Grigs, okay?"

"He doesn't know?"

She shook her head. "And I want to keep it that way. He's a hair away from ending this mission. We can't let that happen, not before we get the runestone."

They approached the Topkapi Palace's Imperial Gate—a marble white structure decorated with Arabic calligraphy. The entrance was set into a brick wall nearly forty feet high, the first of three battlements protecting the treasures inside. Even at this early hour, tourists clustered outside the entrance. News of yesterday's earthquake did little to keep them from their sightseeing schedule.

Grigsby waited outside, sitting on a retaining wall. He tossed a metal, softball-sized orb in his right hand. Strange, Grayle didn't take him for a baseball fan. The elf shoved the orb into his Duster when he saw them coming.

"Howard!" Sarah let go of Grayle's hand and ran to her Caretaker. They hugged long enough for her to whisper why she was calling him Howard.

"You okay?" asked the elf.

She nodded.

"I'm okay too," Grayle added.

Grigsby scowled. "How lucky for us."

"This is Nazan," Sarah said, "the girl who helped us escape the Hagia Sophia."

"Mighty grateful to you, ma'am," Grigsby said, tipping the brim of his hat in her direction. "I know how hard it can be to keep 'er outta trouble."

Sarah punched the elf playfully in the shoulder.

Nazan smiled and bought their entrance tickets from a kiosk. They proceeded through the palace's first courtyard. Sunshine cut between old cypress trees lining the brick pathways. The air was warm, humid, and filled with chirping songbirds. Two octagonal towers capped with conical roofs came into view. The towers flanked the entrance to a second gate.

"Those remind me of the castle towers in Disneyland," Grayle said. "Not that I've ever been to Disneyland, but I've seen pictures."

"They used to hang severed heads from those ramparts," Nazan noted.

Grayle swallowed. "I see, so this *isn't* the happiest place on Earth."

Inside the second courtyard, the pathway split in four directions, radiating outward from the tower gate. They kept to the widest path heading toward the third and final wall.

"The Palace had been the administrative centre of our Empire for five hundred years," Nazan explained. "It was formerly the site of a Roman acropolis. There are still buildings here that date back to Roman times."

"Probably why the Romans feel they have legitimacy to the area," Sarah said.

"Their *legitimacy* is a farce," Nazan grumbled. "That's the Tower of Justice," she said, her voice returning to her tour guide role. She pointed to a tall structure that looked like a church spire. "You can get a great view of the city from up there."

"And those?" Grayle gestured to a row of columns decorating the front of a long building with gray-domed roofs.

"Those were stables for the sultan's horses."

Stables? They looked nicer than the barracks Grayle slept in during his stint at Gloomshroud.

They passed under a gate Nazan described as the Gate of Felicity. It served as the entrance into the sultan's third and most private courtyard and was considered the heart of the palace.

The third courtyard appeared much the same as the first two, with trees and flowers of every color filling well-tended gardens. The only difference was a construction site sectioned off with yellow tape. Men wearing white hard hats climbed up and down a ladder propped inside a hole dug into the cobblestoned walkway.

"We should split up," Grayle suggested once they reached the far end of the courtyard. "That way, we can cover more ground and not be associated with one another, just in case."

"In case of what?" Sarah asked.

"In case one of us gets caught."

"Makes sense," Grigsby agreed.

"And it'll look too suspicious if we only stick to one or two exhibits," Grayle added. "It's best if we go through the entire museum."

Sarah nodded. "I'll take the Sacred Relics exhibit. Howard, you take the Harem."

Grigsby grimaced, either at being called Howard again or at being given orders.

"Nazan and I will take the Treasury," Grayle said. He gave Sarah a knowing look. *Keep your enemies closer.*

"Remember, photography is prohibited," Nazan reminded them. "We'll have to commit what we see to memory." She glanced at the time on her cell phone. "We'll meet back here in an hour. Agreed?"

Everyone nodded and went their separate ways.

* * *

Sarah watched the others weave through the growing number of tourists entering the courtyard. Her attention lingered on Grayle as he and Nazan made their way to the Treasury. The reality of what she was asking—not asking, manipulating—him to do hit home again.

She had wanted to tell him about the bounty on his head, especially after he'd taken her hand. It was a sweet gesture—a tenderness that didn't often peek through his otherwise abrasive personality. She imagined he wouldn't be so tender when he discovered there was a price on his head.

She sighed. *I can't keep him in the dark forever.* He'll find out about the bounty eventually. And when he did, what then? Would he panic, abandon the mission? *He's too invested in finding the Eye to back out now.*

Still, she couldn't take that risk.

Grayle's importance to the mission was undeniable. She wouldn't be able to find the runestones without him. But he was more to her than just a means to an end, wasn't he?

Sarah sighed, then made her way across the marbled courtyard to the Sacred Relics exhibit.

Whatever feelings she had for him, she couldn't let her emotions influence her objective. Finding the Eye was all that mattered. It had to come first before anything, or anyone, else.

Chapter 27

S ebastian Caine stared at the monitors arranged on flat surfaces throughout his posh penthouse suite. Each screen flashed with real time intel fed through his communications satellite and beamed to his location.

After his Crusaders lost the witch and Hexhunter in the Hagia Sophia, Caine was quick to have his techs hack every surveillance camera in the city. He couldn't be sure the two teenagers and their Caretaker had left the city—he just had a feeling they hadn't.

He'd been right again.

His surveillance systems found a match to Sarah Finn five minutes ago. It had taken some time. Caine saw why.

The girl disguised herself. Smart.

But Caine's tracking software was sophisticated. It took height, weight, body structure, even thermal imaging patterns into account in order to locate a person. When the software found its closest match, Finn was already moving through the Topkapi Palace gardens.

No sign of the Hexhunter though—as Caine expected.

During their failed attempt to steal the runestone from the Vancouver Museum, he discovered Rowen could not be seen by conventional cameras, digital or otherwise. Until their encounter yesterday, Caine had never seen the Hexhunter up close. He memorized the boy's features, the frightened but determined look on his face, his body moving with surprising speed and agility.

If I had those reflexes, I could have jumped clear of the chandelier, Caine thought. He escaped the falling fixture relatively unscathed. His leg had been pinned, but luckily no broken bones. Only bruises.

He remembered the feral look in Sarah Finn's eyes. She wanted to kill him. He thought the witch lacked the conviction to do what was necessary in order to avenge her mother's death. Apparently he'd been wrong. If it weren't for Rowen's intervention, would she have gone through with it? *He* never showed restraint or remorse when it came to killing; why should she be any different? Yet it bothered him that she had the opportunity to exact her vengeance in the first place.

Hel had her pinned to the scaffold—she was easy prey. What went wrong?

The security guard.

He came out of nowhere, taking out Mussels and two of his commandos. He'd also pumped three bullets into Hel.

Iron bullets?

If that were the case, the guard knew about Folklore. Only iron could neutralize Folklorians, whether they be witches, monsters, or deities.

Whoever the stranger was, he may have done him a favor.

But is Hel dead?

Caine focused back on the video screens. Sarah Finn was well inside the palace before the recognition software caught her image.

The Hexhunter had been next to her, hiding her from sight until now.

"She's going into the Sacred Relics exhibit," said David Strauss. The handsome tech's face filled one of the monitors to Caine's left. "What do you suppose she's doing?"

Caine drummed his fingers on the tabletop. "Definitely not sightseeing," he replied. "What treasures does the Palace contain?"

Keys tapped as Strauss searched. "We have various holy artifacts, weapons, jewels—"

"Anything of Folklore origin?"

More typing.

Strauss pressed his lips together and shook his head. "The data is spotty as far as the Ottoman Folklore is concerned. No artifacts of Viking origin are on record either."

That had been Caine's next question.

"What are the sorcière and Hexhunter doing there then?" Mussels asked. A harsh purple welt swelled on his forehead. The security guard's baton had struck the bodyguard with uncanny precision.

"Whatever it is, it must be linked to another piece of Mimir's Stone. How old is this footage?" Caine asked.

Strauss glanced at the timestamp on his screen. "Three minutes."

"Good. That still gives us time."

The computer analyst raised an eyebrow. "Time for what?"

"Not your concern." Caine leaned forward and disconnected the link between them. The monitor went dark.

Mussels lumbered to where his employer sat. "What's our move, Chef?"

"We go to the Topkapi Palace. Prep the helicopter and inform the mercenaries to prepare for another assault."

"Armed?"

Caine nodded. "Full Crusader gear. The Hexhunter will be ours this time."

Chapter 28

Sarah spotted the first security camera when she entered the Sacred Relics' threshold. It was set high in the corner, whirring silently from side to side. Maybe it was all in her head, but she could've sworn the lens zoomed in on her. How many had been following her movements since entering the Palace?

Stop being so paranoid. Everything'll be fine.

But thinking the words didn't stop her growing unease. She decided to examine the Holy Banner, then grab Grayle and Grigsby and get the heck out of there.

She made her way through the displays in the first room, keeping her distance from security guards circling the exhibit like vultures. The space was filled with glass cases protecting pieces of tattered holy books, shrines, weapons, even the foot impressions and bone fragments of holy figures. A human arm, fashioned entirely of brass, encased the desiccated limb of a prophet. A small portion of the brass was open so visitors could see the holy bones tucked inside.

Stepping into the next room, Sarah came upon a solitary golden box set on a pedestal. It held what was supposed to be the Blessed

Mantle of Muhammad, a cloak said to be two yards long and made of black wool lined with a cream-colored fabric. According to the artifact's description, if a button on the mantle was dipped in rose water, its drops were claimed to have miraculous healing qualities.

Interesting, but still not what Sarah was looking for.

She found the banner in the third room, hanging in a case beneath a gold-latticed canopy. It was nothing more than a large black cloth, a part of a tent or an unravelled turban.

How did something so simple end up with magical powers? Sarah wondered. After a year of retrieving relics just like this, she was still amazed how the most unassuming artifacts were imbued with hidden powers. Nazan's cousin, Yusuf, had said that whoever carried the banner into battle would triumph over his or her enemies. He didn't seem convinced of the artifact's powers. Sarah wasn't either. She couldn't read an aura from the fabric.

Had the original been lost or stolen? Maybe replaced with a replica?

She dropped her mental guard further, trying to connect with her Auralex senses, see if the banner was truly authentic. Something dulled her link to the ambient energy. She scanned the room. Metal shutters, elegantly carved into floral patterns, covered the windows. They must have been made from iron—one of two elements that withered a witch's powers. Salt was the other.

Sarah couldn't get a reading through the interference. She *did* feel a sudden flash of hostility, however. Focused on the banner, she never noticed the four men, arms crossed and ready for business, gathering at the entrance of the third room. Their attention was directed toward her.

Had someone tipped them off? Caine? The Ottomans?

Caine would have come after me himself. And why would the Ottomans have us steal their artifacts only to have us captured?

It didn't make sense.

Unless the Ottomans discovered who I am.

The thought sent a chill down Sarah's spine. If they knew who she was, that meant they knew of the warrant for her arrest. And if they were aware of *her*, did they know about Grayle?

Her eyes darted to the ceiling. More cameras monitored this part of the exhibit—two in opposite corners, covering the whole room.

Someone could have been tracking me this whole time.

Another four guards appeared at the entrance, using their bodies to barricade the way out.

Sarah wanted to avoid a confrontation at all costs. Finding a means of escape was always preferable to combat, especially when she was outnumbered eight to one. She scanned the room for another way out. There was none. Small, stained-glass windows circled the ceiling above her. Too high to reach, even with magic. Those windows that were within crashing-through distance were reinforced with the iron shutters. They drained her magic *and* prevented her escape. Not that magic was an option with Outlanders around. A young couple in their twenties were the in the room with her. Sarah couldn't risk exposing her powers in front of them.

"You will not reveal your powers while in the presence of Outlanders"—it was one of the Coven's most sacred rules. Then again, Sarah had broken their rules before, what was one more? *And with a warrant out for my arrest, how much worse off will I be?*

Satisfied with their tour of the room's collection, the young couple squeezed past the men lingering at the exit.

Only Sarah and the eight Roman security guards remained.

No Outlanders. No witnesses. No broken rules.

That suited her just fine.

Sarah unraveled her pashmina and stuffed the fabric in her pants pocket. The disguise was useless now. It would only get in the way in the coming fight.

She reached deep down, slowed her breathing, and willed her magic to flare. She wrapped her mind around the sensation, letting the vibe thrum through her body. Her muscles pulsed, ready to spring, pounce, kick, punch, throw—do anything to make it out to freedom.

Then four more guards emerged behind the others. Eight had turned to twelve.

Sarah swallowed. *Way too many.*

"You need to come with us," one of the guards said.

Sarah's fingers curled into fists. "What if I refuse?"

A dozen hands reached for billy clubs strapped to their belts.

"Okay then," Sarah said. Her hands ignited blue. "Come and get me."

Chapter 29

Grayle went to work memorizing the Treasury's layout as soon as he and Nazan stepped inside. A quick glance revealed some troubling developments. The room was much smaller than he anticipated. There was only one door and no windows. The walls were bare except for a dozen porcelain vases in a glass-fronted display case to his far left. Leafed gold tiles in the shape of shrinking fish scales covered the ceiling. The pattern was interrupted by a single vent, too high to reach.

Most of the exhibit's treasures were arranged on pedestals and glass casings in the middle of the room. The largest group of tourists surrounded the Spoonmaker's Diamond. They ooed and awed over the priceless, drop-shaped gem as it sparkled inside its protective case.

"Beautiful, don't you think?" Nazan gushed beside him.

Set in silver, the eighty-six carat diamond, the fourth largest in the world, was framed by forty-nine smaller diamonds.

Grayle shrugged. Beauty and craftsmanship didn't interest him—the value did. And the security measures meant to protect them.

He circled the velvet ropes intended to keep visitors at arm's length from the artifact. He noted the slight discoloration in the tiles surrounding the base of the glass case. They were newer and more polished than the others.

Pressure plates.

A step too close and alarms would go off.

"Do you believe Butrus' story, that the fisherman who found the diamond was swindled into believing it was a worthless piece of glass?" Grayle asked.

It was Nazan's turn to shrug. "Many stories the elders tell are passed on to provide lessons."

"Like don't trust anyone?"

"Perhaps that not all things are as they appear to be," she said. "So how long have you and Brenna been together?"

The question took Grayle by surprise. "A few months," he lied. It had only been three days, not counting the two weeks he and Sarah saw one another in Bayview's hallways.

"Where did you meet?" Nazan asked.

Why was she asking questions? Was she curious or fishing for information?

"Midgard," Grayle answered.

"Alistair isn't a typical Norse name."

"That's because I'm not Norse."

"Where are you from?"

That was the million dollar question.

"The Celtic Folklore. My father's a merchant. We were in Midgard selling our merchandise."

"What does he sell?"

"Cell phones."

Nazan scrunched her face. "Cell phones?"

"The Vikings are some of our best customers. They have a habit of smashing things, especially whatever happens to be in their hand, which these days is their cell phones."

Nazan smiled. "Well, you two seem good together. From what I understand, it's rare for a magicker to have relationships with a Mundy."

Mundy? Was that short for a mundane...someone who was non-magical?

Grayle had no clue there were rules when it came to witches having relationships. Then again, it made sense. How could a person with magical powers be interested in someone normal? Wouldn't it be boring?

"Sorry. I talk a lot when I'm nervous," Nazan admitted as the silence between them grew awkward. "I've never done anything like *this* before."

"Planned a heist?" Grayle whispered. "Not many have."

"Have you?" she asked.

"There's nothing to be nervous about," he said, purposely dodging the question. "Let's finish our survey here and figure out how we're going to steal them later."

He moved on to a mannequin to his left. It was dressed in a rich, plain white tunic, complete with bright red, Keebler elf shoes that curled up at the toes. The Emerald Dagger was strapped to the mannequin's chest. It glittered with its mix of gold, diamonds, and emeralds. Both dagger and mannequin were secured in a glass case.

From his training at Gloomshroud, Grayle knew this kind of hardened glass was heated and cooled several times, making it ten times stronger than regular glass. The edges were also reinforced with metal strips. No way to get in without either lifting or smashing it.

And if we do get the Dagger, there's still the matter of keeping it from the Ottomans, and then using it to open a tomb we don't know where to find.

Sudden movements reflected in the glass shifted Grayle's attention. Five guards gathered near the exit, speaking in hushed voices.

Grayle's ears perked. Nervous chatter from radios attached to their shoulders alerted him something was wrong.

He scanned around him nervously. *Are they on to me?*

Four of the five guards hurried away, leaving only one to protect the entrance.

Grayle frowned. Whatever was happening didn't concern him.

His pulse quickened.

Sarah.

He moved to the exit, not too quick to arouse suspicion, but fast enough to beat other tourists to the door.

"What is it?" Nazan asked behind him.

Grayle didn't answer.

They followed palace security at a discreet distance. Somehow Grayle knew where they'd be going—the Sacred Relics exhibit. A small crowd had formed, gravitating to the unrest. Tourists gawked as a girl was led across the palace courtyard, arms restrained, escorted by eight guards.

Grayle stopped behind a marble column. *Quite the overkill for a regular teenager. They must have found out she's a witch.*

Looking closer, he spotted Sarah sporting new bruises and a fat lip. Several guards had injuries of their own. One limped, while another had a nasty gash across his forehead. All of them had burn marks and rips in their uniforms.

Grigsby came up next to Grayle. "What happened?" he asked.

"Don't know," Grayle replied, not taking his eyes off Sarah.

"Thirty minutes in and she's captured?" Nazan hissed. "I thought you two knew what you were doing. We have to get out of here."

She turned to leave.

"I'm not going anywhere without her," Grayle said.

"Girlfriend or not, Brenna's a casualty now. It'll be too dangerous to get her out. Let our negotiators arrange her release."

Grayle shook his head. "No. We might be able to save her and get the artifacts at the same time."

"The same time? Are you crazy? The Romans are reviewing their video feeds by now, tracking Brenna's movements through the palace. They will see we came with her."

They won't see me, Grayle thought. "We'll never get another chance like this," he said firmly.

"I can't believe I'm sayin' this, but I'm with the kid," Grigsby muttered. "We gotta do it now before the Romans call in the cavalry."

Nazan's eyes narrowed, clearly disliking the idea. "Fine," she relented. "But there is no way we can steal all three."

"No, but we can get one. The dagger."

She frowned. "Why the dagger?"

Because I need it to open a hidden tomb, Grayle wanted to say. "It's the easiest of the three," he said instead.

Nazan blew out a breath. "Do you know what the Romans will do to us if we are caught? They will drag us behind chariots, boil us alive, or—"

"That won't happen, not if you do exactly what I say." Grayle watched as the guards and Sarah disappeared around the corner. "Do you know where they're taking her?"

"There is a small jail in the eastern corner of the courtyard, behind the administrative buildings. They're probably taking her there."

Grayle faced Grigsby. "Can you free her?" he asked.

"Does a one-legged duck swim in a circle?"

"I'll take that as a yes." Grayle turned back to Nazan. "Can you get us out of here, out of the Palace?"

Her brow furrowed. "I-I might."

"Might or you *can*?"

She put her hands on her hips. "I can."

"Good, because we're going to need a quick exit."

"What're you plannin', kid?" Grigsby asked.

"Have you ever heard of a smash and grab?"

Chapter 30

Brenna took care choosing where she stepped. Weeds grew wild along the ramparts, sprouting between cobblestones, making them loose and brittle. The last thing she needed was a twisted ankle. The pitch grew steeper as the Midgard's walls meandered higher up the mountainside. The fortifications were swallowed by a layer of velvet clouds and dark forest closer to the summit. Beyond the wall's edge to her left, Idun Falls thundered in full force. It was choked with boulders, and the water bubbled white and frothy as it found its way into the fjord four hundred feet below.

Brenna took a deep breath. The fresh scent of pine and wet moss lingered in the air. Her connection with the ambient energy always felt stronger in the wilderness. She could sense a fox foraging for food nearby, the powerful presence of a bear, and birds darting among the evergreens.

Her senses touched Hrafn circling overhead. The crow had followed her up the slope, occasionally landing on a branch to rest and squawk at her.

More pork? the crow would ask.

Brenna ran out of treats a half hour ago, but that didn't stop Hrafn from checking every five minutes.

"Sorry. You'll have to wait until we get home," she said patiently.

The crow screeched his disappointment.

Brenna continued inspecting the wall as she hiked, searching for weaknesses that Hel or the traitor may have exploited. She saw nothing. Not that she knew what she was looking for. A hole in the wall? A sign that said: *Hel breached the defenses here?*

Midgard hadn't seen an attack in three hundred years, not since the last great battle against Ymir, the Jotun king. Since then, the guards kept vigil along the fjord—the most likely place for an attack.

Brenna's temper simmered. *And no one had the foresight that maybe someone could infiltrate our defenses somewhere else?*

She took out her phone, hoping some hilarious cat videos would cool her frustration.

"*Hrodi,*" she cursed. Youtube was buffering endlessly.

She switched to searching the internet instead. She was about to cross-reference *"capitals of the east"* with *"Varangians"* when she hesitated. Were her searches still being monitored? If that were the case, investigating anything to do with *Varangians* could give Sarah's location away.

I could search different "capitals of the east", throw Malin off her scent.

Brenna typed Kiev into the search field as she walked, left it on the webpage for a few minutes, and was about to search Istanbul when she thought back to her phone conversation with Sarah. Normally, Brenna's focus would have been on Sarah's face—those blue eyes, the arched eyebrows, and that gorgeous raven hair any girl would die for. But there was something behind Sarah—gold script embossed on a black, circular plaque. They weren't letters— at least not any that Brenna recognized. They weren't runes either.

The writing looked Arabic.

That left Baghdad or Istanbul. Both cities had been *capitals of the east* in the past. And both were in Arabic countries.

Brenna knew it was only a matter of time before Malin and Folklorian agents found Sarah.

If she and the Hexhunter were smart, they'd lay low—not draw attention to themselves.

Witches who opposed the Coven and broke Wiccan laws rarely escaped punishment. They were stripped of their positions and imprisoned for their crimes. In extreme cases, some had their ability to wield magic forcibly removed—a kind of magic lobotomy.

Brenna shivered.

Few witches survived the procedure.

Hrafn squawked from above. *We here.*

Brenna put away her phone.

A mighty rock formation stretched high above the wall's outer edge to her left. The Pillar of Halvor was a natural carved thrust of gray granite rising high and independent of the mountainside. Too thick to cut through, the wall skirted around its rocky foundation.

She stepped closer, feeling tired and disoriented. Was her lack of sleep finally getting to her? Was it exhaustion from the climb? Or was she drained from not having breakfast this morning?

No. This feels different.

Hrafn screeched from a treetop to her right.

Strange. Her thoughts were muddled, murky. She couldn't get a clear read on what he was saying.

"I don't have any food left," she told him again.

The ramparts spun beneath her feet, causing her to stumble.

Something was wrong.

Hrafn screeched a second time. His head was stretched forward, wings splayed aggressively behind him.

Brenna stopped.

That had nothing to do with pork. It was a warning.

She heard the faint crunch of gravel behind her.

I'm not alone.

Her hand tightened around the hilt of her sword.

"Svein, you're about as good at stalking as you are at babysitting."

She drew her sword in one smooth motion and swung around, thrusting the blade in front of her.

It wasn't Svein.

Chapter 31

S arah prowled her jail cell like a caged tiger. End to end, stone wall to iron bars. The metal should have sapped her strength, but something kept pumping energy into her limbs.

Was it the fear of what might happen next?

Concern for Grayle?

Desperation to find the runestone?

Or was it her anger at getting caught?

Less than twenty-four hours between discovering there was a warrant for my arrest and actually getting caught. Must be a new record.

She turned and slid down the stone wall. Her laptop bag lay in the far corner, flung out of reach. Things could be worse. She thanked the Norns that Grayle wasn't occupying any of the cells next to her, or that Wicca Malin hadn't arrived yet.

The main door to the cellblock opened.

Sarah reached out with her Auralex senses, trying to penetrate the iron barrier. It was useless. Too much interference. She relied on her ears instead.

Three people, she guessed by the number of footfalls echoing down the corridor.

She stood and leaned against the wall, arms crossed. She wasn't about to let her captors see her huddled and afraid.

A balding man appeared, shadowed by a security guard. Sarah spotted the SPQR tattoos on each of their forearms: *Senatus Populus Que Romanus*—The Senate and the People of Rome.

Hamza stood with them, a coin pouch clutched in his hand. His gold tooth flashed as he gave her a smug smile.

"Is this her?" asked the balding man. He seemed to be the one in charge.

Hamza nodded. "That's her."

Sarah wished shooting laser beams from her eyeballs was one of her powers. The traitor would've been a puddle of goo.

"Very well." The balding man gave a slight nod.

The guard beside Hamza slipped a baton from his belt and clubbed the snitch over the head. Hamza cried out and crumpled to the floor, out cold.

"So you're Sarah Finn, daughter of the great Rachel Finn," said the balding man, unfazed by the sudden attack. "My name is Varius Claudius Scaeva, the Praetor of this district." He looked more like an accountant than a Roman official. "I apologize for the meagre accommodations, but we are somewhat limited here at the Palace."

The Roman's voice barely registered. Sarah was focused on the guard as he plucked the coin pouch from Hamza's hand, then grabbed him by the legs and dragged him out of sight.

Varius snapped his fingers, diverting Sarah's attention back on him. "Upon learning of your presence at the Palace, we doubled the security in our exhibits."

"Who's Sarah Finn?" she asked innocently.

Varius examined her critically. His close-set eyes stared down a long nose. "You should be more selective with who you ally yourself with," he said, deciding to ignore her attempt at deception. "The Ottomans are a treacherous lot. Learning of the warrant for your arrest, they were quick to notify us—with the understanding that we would give them certain concessions as a reward for your capture."

A jail cell door clanged shut, and the guard returned to Varius' side.

"Sadly, they'll get neither," the Praetor continued. "Even though money is of no consequence to the Empire, information *is*. The warrant failed to mention why you were to be apprehended. Perhaps you could enlighten me."

Sarah stared at the man, saying nothing.

Varius nodded to the guard. He stepped forward, unlocking the jail cell door.

Sarah uncrossed her arms and backed away. Her heartbeat quickened. She knew the attack on Hamza served as an example of what might happen if she didn't cooperate. Still, she wasn't about to spill her guts.

The guard ducked inside, the two-and-a-half foot long baton still clenched in his hand. He was six feet tall with forearms the size of her legs. Stubble surrounded his thick jawline, and his hooked nose showed evidence of being broken several times.

"I would prefer we not have to resort to unpleasantries," Varius said, "but I need you to provide me with the information."

The guard moved within striking distance.

Sarah judged her ability to overwhelm him. Her chances weren't good. In the confined space, she wouldn't have much room to maneuver. And the iron bars still dulled her magic. She would have to rely solely on hand-to-hand combat.

Would a swift kick to the groin or a chop to the Adam's apple cripple him?

She didn't think so. The man was built like a tank.

Varius grew impatient. "Your reluctance gives me concern, young witch. Perhaps some motivation will set your mind to task." He nodded to the guard.

The baton came swinging. Hot pain exploded as the weapon whacked Sarah just above the knee. She sucked air through her teeth.

"I will ask you again, why has the Supreme Coven put a warrant out for your arrest?"

Sarah shifted her weight off her throbbing leg. "I went off script…on my last mission," she said, eyes fixed on the guard. Her answer was partly true. She *had* gone "off script"—not returning to Midgard after Baldersted, refusing to turn over a suspected Hexhunter, and pursuing the Eye of Odin without the Coven's permission.

"That's not the *whole* truth though, is it?" Varius concluded.

"That's the truth. They're PO'd because I never reported in. They think I've gone rogue."

The Roman wasn't convinced. "Why would they think that…unless you have something they want?" Another gesture sent the guard's baton swinging again, this time catching Sarah between the shoulder and bicep muscle.

She cried out. "Okay-okay, I have gone rogue." She cradled her arm as it went numb. "I'm retrieving artifacts and keeping them for myself. Can you blame me? I can get more money by selling the relics than returning them to their rightful Folklores."

The answer seemed to appease Varius. "What were you planning on stealing?"

Sarah had to think quickly.

The guard raised his baton.

"I was going to steal the Holy Banner," she said. "Any Ottoman or religious fanatic would spend a fortune for it."

"And how were you planning to come to such a prize?"

"I didn't get that far. I was casing the Sacred Relics exhibit when you caught me."

The Praetor's lips pressed into a thin line. "Who else are you working with?"

"No one. I work alone. Don't have to share the profits that way."

She had to be careful not to implicate Grayle or make Varius aware of his presence in the palace.

Varius took a moment to consider her story. "I believe you are speaking the truth," he finally said. "But the truth also confirms your guilt. You were going to steal from the Empire and must be punished accordingly. Ten strikes should do it," he said to the baton-wielding guard inside the cell. "Then keep her confined until the Wicca—"

At that moment, a metal cylinder bounced down the corridor. With a metallic clink, it rolled and came to a stop at Varius' feet.

Sarah recognized its elvish design. One of Grigsby's flash bombs.

She had just enough time to squeeze her eyes shut and plug her ears before the device exploded. With a thundering whomp, a shockwave forced the air from Sarah's lungs and sent both her and the Roman guard slamming against the cell wall. The guard's crushing weight landed on top of her. Sarah laid there, her ears ringing, eyesight blurry.

She could make out Grigsby's muffled voice as he stepped over an unconscious Varius. "I knew this heist was goin' to be a bad idea."

Sarah heaved the unconscious guard off and got onto her shaky legs. The room spun like a bifrost. She braced herself on the jail cell wall, waiting for the world to stop spinning. Slowly, it did. She staggered out and threw her arms around the elf. "Where's Grayle? Is he safe?"

"He's gone to steal the dagger."

"We have to stop him." She picked up her laptop bag stuffed in the corner. "The Ottomans betrayed us. There's a warrant for our arrest."

Grigs raised his voice. "There's a what-now?"

Sarah stumbled down the corridor. "Wicca Malin is on her way. She put out a warrant for my arrest and a bounty on Grayle's head." She caught the elf's disapproving glare. "I know, I know. We can discuss my impulsiveness another time—"

"We *will*, you can count on that," Grigs assured her.

"—but right now, *Grayle* is all that matters."

They exited the cellblock.

The palace grounds were bustling with tourists strolling leisurely through the gardens. Some stopped to take photos of the palace's grand architecture. Guards patrolled not only the entrances to exhibits, but vigilantly marched up and down the courtyard.

Grigsby reached for his Winchester.

"Keep it holstered, cowboy," Sarah said. She hoped there wouldn't be a need to use it, especially with so many Outlanders around. "You have to get back to the *Drakkar* and get her ready to launch."

"I ain't leavin' you again," the Caretaker argued.

"We'll need a quick escape out of the city. Malin might be here by now. We can't let her take Grayle."

"Yer riskin' too much for that boy."

"It's worth it if it keeps the Eye out of Caine's and Hel's hands," Sarah countered. "Get the *Drakkar* ready. We'll be there soon." She put a hand on his arm. "I need you to do this."

Grigsby squeezed her to him, then held her at arm's length so he could look into her eyes. "Don't do anything stupid," he said and hurried for the courtyard gate.

Sarah turned toward the Treasury. Retrieving the artifacts would be all but impossible now. Escape was their priority. Until someone checked on Varius, no one would know she'd escaped. The Praetor had gotten the brunt of flash bomb's blast. He and the guard would be out of commission for at least another ten or fifteen minutes.

If we're quiet and don't draw attention to ourselves, we can sneak out before anyone suspects a thing.

That's when a high-pitched alarm began to wail.

Chapter 32

The plan was stupid, and Grayle knew it.

He'd had a lot of hair-brained schemes over the years, but a smash and grab inside a fortified palace took the prize.

He stared at the thick tempered glass case. Inside, propped on the dummy dressed in Sultan's garb, was the Emerald Dagger.

Everything depended on him getting it—their hunt for the Eye, keeping the world safe, discovering where he came from.

There was no plan B.

Nazan stood next to him, arms crossed, her right foot tapping nervously on the tile floor.

"Relax," he whispered. "You're going to draw attention to us."

Her foot went still. "How can I relax? This is crazy!"

Yeah. It was crazy—even though the plan itself was simple: smash the glass, grab the dagger, escape. No expertise or finesse was required. Not that Grayle oozed finesse. But even he favored a skillful challenge rather than the sheer idiocy of what he was about to do.

Three obstacles stood in their way: the tempered glass casing, three walled-in courtyards, and a growing number of security gathering inside the exhibit.

Did the Romans suspect Sarah wasn't working alone?

One thing was certain, the longer he and Nazan stayed here, the more suspicious the guards would become. They had to steal the dagger now. But how? The glass was too thick to smash by hand.

C'mon, Grayle. Think.

At Gloomshroud Camp for Delinquent Youth, he learned any number of objects could break reinforced glass—from the obvious, like bullets, an axe, or a sledgehammer, to the more obscure. Spark plugs from a car engine, for example, could shatter tempered windshields. It had something to do with the mix of metal and porcelain that...

Porcelain.

Grayle's eyes shot to the accent wall on the far side of the room. Rows of vases gleamed inside, each inlaid with gold and silver—all were made of porcelain.

A new plan began to take shape, one still on the verge of stupidity...

But it could give us a fighting chance to pull this off.

He leaned in closer to Nazan. "I need you to go over there, to the vases."

She raised a nervous eyebrow. "Why?"

"On my signal, you're going to smash the glass and throw me a vase."

"What!" She had the look of a scared five-year-old right then.

"I'm going to use a vase to break the casing," Grayle explained.

She stared at him, open-mouthed. "What makes you think a *vase* can break it?"

"Something I learned."

"Where?"

"Nevermind that." Explaining his criminal credentials would take too long. Besides, he was supposed to be the son of a merchant from the Celtic Folklore, not some mysterious orphan who also happened to be a thief and Hexhunter. "Trust me," he added. "I've done this before." *Well…not quite something like this*, he reminded himself.

"I-I don't—I don't think I can do it," Nazan stammered.

Grayle sighed. They didn't have time for indecision. "Look, you want the dagger or not?"

"How am I going to smash the glass?"

He gently removed the shawl from her head. A mass of black curls sprang loose. He wrapped the fabric around her hand. "Give it a good swing."

Her face went ghostly pale. She opened her mouth.

Grayle cut her off before she could argue. "On my signal," he repeated. "Go."

He watched her walk stiffly to the wall mount, hands clenched into fists. He hoped his plan worked.

A noise echoed outside—rhythmic and distant.

A helicopter?

The thumping grew louder.

Grayle's internal alarm started going off again. He doubted helicopters were allowed to land in the palace grounds.

So what's going on?

The noise drew everyone's attention to the courtyard. Security guards left their post to see what was happening outside.

Worst. Guards. Ever, Grayle thought. But he couldn't waste this opportunity.

He waited until a cluster of tourists cleared the space between him and Nazan.

Now, he mouthed to her.

The girl hesitated, biting her lip and twisting the fabric wrapped around her hand. Grayle could tell she was on the verge of a mental breakdown.

Her second thoughts could ruin everything.

"Now!" he yelled.

The shout startled everyone in the room. It also jolted Nazan into action.

She balled her hand and swung at the glass. But the hammer fist was too tentative, only hard enough to rattle the glass in its frame.

Tourists froze, unsure what the girl was doing.

"Dur!" the remaining guard shouted. He moved toward her, slowly at first, then faster.

Seeing the guard coming must have steeled Nazan's nerves. She swung at the display harder. This time, the plate glass broke. Large shards splintered and tumbled to the tile floor with a loud crash.

"Dur! Prohibere!" the guard shouted above the blare of whooping alarms. Tourists gasped, clearing a way as he bolted toward her.

Nazan grabbed the first vase she could reach and, without aiming, lobbed it in Grayle's direction.

It was a sloppy toss.

Grayle ran and slid on the polished marble as though he were skidding for home plate. He caught the vase in both hands before it shattered.

A few tourists cheered his effort to save the priceless porcelain. Their praise was short lived.

Grayle got to his feet, grabbed the artifact by the neck, and swung. He instinctively shut his eyes from the showering splinters as the porcelain exploded against the Emerald Dagger's glass casing. When he opened them again, the tempered glass had cracked at the point of impact, but that was it. Nothing else happened.

You've got to be kidding me.

In a last ditch effort, Grayle heel-kicked the casing. Like snapping ice, cracks spider-webbed across the glass. The casing ruptured all at once, sending shards cascading onto the marble floor. Grayle reached up and yanked the dagger off the mannequin.

Smash and grab complete, Grayle bolted to where Nazan still struggled with the guard. Managing to wriggle an arm free, she grabbed another vase and smashed it over his head. The guard sank dazed to the floor.

Grayle took her hand and pulled her toward the exit. Thankfully none of the tourists played the hero and tried to stop them as they rushed through the exhibit. He shoved aside those who got too close.

The missing guards emerged just as Grayle and Nazan were about to make their exit.

The alarm must have sent them running back to their posts. Like a wall of linebackers, they blocked any chance of escape.

There was nothing Grayle could do. He knew when he was outmatched, outnumbered and out of luck.

Chapter 33

Sarah's arm and leg still ached where the Roman guard had whacked her, but at least the effects of the flash bomb were beginning to wear off. The ringing in her ears was replaced by the sound of a helicopter hovering overhead and the alarm blaring with a high-pitched wail.

Sarah ignored the noise, pushing her way through the growing crowd in front of the Treasury. Security rushing to the exhibit drew in curious onlookers and, at the same time, chased away those sensing trouble. Six guards blocked the entrance, their attention focused inward.

Sarah mustered her magic. Raw energy surged from her core, growing outward, filling every molecule until her skin seemed to vibrate.

Her senses touched the Crusader assassin.

He's somewhere in the courtyard.

She couldn't let his presence distract her. How much time did she have until Varius regained consciousness and alerted the palace she'd escaped?

Sarah didn't care how many Outlanders were watching. Time was running out. Feeling her power spike, she released the magic with a single word: "Vanya!"

The pulse wave projected like an invisible force, plowing into the security guards, knocking them senseless against the marble walls and into each other. A single guard remained standing, dazed and wobbling like a spare bowling pin. Sarah had hoped for a strike.

She was about to unleash another pulse to finish the job when she saw Grayle charging from inside. He rushed the lone guard, using his momentum to cannon into the larger man. The guard tripped and went down hard. Grayle was clear, Nazan close at his heels.

Sarah dashed to his side, spying the Emerald Dagger in his hand.

"How do we get out of here?" Grayle looked expectantly at Nazan.

A quick scan of the courtyard revealed few options. The gates had been closed when the alarm had gone off.

"I don't—I don't—" the girl sputtered.

"I thought you said you could get us out of here!" Grayle shouted.

Nazan's body tensed. "I didn't expect alarms to be going off and *that* being here!"

She pointed at the roaring helicopter hovering thirty feet above them. The downdraft from the rotor blades shook tree limbs and sent dust, leaves, and debris swirling in the courtyard. Its cabin door slid open. Ropes unfurled, dropping to the ground. Mercenaries dressed in black military fatigue rappelled from the craft. Silver crosses reflected off their bulletproof vests.

Sarah spied the worksite they had passed earlier. "This way."

They dashed for the yellow construction tape thirty yards away. "If we can't go over the palace walls—we go under them." She turned to Nazan running alongside her. "The cisterns. You said the waterways criss-cross under the city, right? Even under the palace?"

The girl nodded, her eyes wide as dinner plates.

They ducked under the construction tape. A metal ladder was propped inside a gaping hole dug into the sidewalk.

Shouts erupted behind them. Six Romans sprinted from the right. Five Crossers came from the left, automatic weapons raised.

Grayle tucked the dagger into his waistband and stepped onto the first rung. "Down we go," he said, disappearing into the darkness. Nazan went after him.

Sarah stopped, catching a glimpse of Caine inside the helicopter's cockpit. His eyes were hidden behind his trademark sunglasses. Anger ignited inside Sarah like a flame, the same anger she felt back at the Hagia Sophia. She clenched her fists, digging her nails into her palms.

"Sarah! C'mon!" Grayle yelled from below.

She tore her eyes away.

Revenge would have to wait.

The ladder rattled as Sarah climbed down. She was about to tug the ladder from the opening when the first Roman appeared. He grabbed the other end. They struggled, playing tug-o-war for several seconds. Then, rather than pulling, Sarah thrust the ladder upward, knocking the Roman's front teeth out. The man howled, loosening his grip. She forced the ladder from his hands and tossed it out of reach.

"C'mon," Grayle said.

They splashed in ankle high water, following the cistern tunnel deeper under the palace.

* * *

The Operative watched from afar as the Hexhunter, witch, and some girl climbed into the construction pit. He was about to go after them when six palace guards disappeared into the same hole. Five mercenaries followed a minute later, armed with M16s and grenades. They meant business this time.

The Operative wasn't about to go in after them. Going underground outnumbered eleven to one was tactically unsound.

Still, he couldn't stand idly by and do nothing. It wasn't in his nature.

The Inner Circle wanted him to cause less interference, be even less conspicuous than before. Following those orders was difficult when your adversary came roaring in with a helicopter. He was willing to follow their orders, let events play out with minimal involvement on his part, unless the two teenagers were in trouble.

Like now.

He stroked his chin, thinking what his next move should be.

Caine jumped out of the helicopter the moment the landing skids touched ground. Mussels hopped out after him. They hurried inside the Treasury.

To discover what the Hexhunter had stolen, the Operative presumed.

He eyed the lone helicopter pilot checking his gauges inside the aircraft. He appeared to be the Operative's height and build.

The Operative smiled.

Perfect.

* * *

The light of the construction opening quickly grew fainter as Sarah, Grayle, and Nazan sloshed down the cistern's main shaft.

Sarah held out her hand. "Naur-galad." A fireball hovered inches above her palm, illuminating the cavern ahead. Wet slime coated the tunnel walls. A rat darted from the light, seeking shadows to hide in.

At least it isn't a sewer, Sarah thought thankfully. "Do you know where these tunnels will take us?" she asked.

Nazan shook her head. "They criss-cross under the palace and throughout most of Istanbul. You can go from one end of the old city to the next without having to step foot on the surface."

That didn't help much. If they re-emerged while still in the palace compound, they would most likely be caught. The Palace would be on lockdown by now. No one in or out until everyone was thoroughly searched. The only thing to do was keep going.

The tunnel sloped gently downward for the next forty yards, the stonework slick beneath their feet. They inched along cautiously, testing the slippery surface as they descended. Water spilled into a large basin ahead of them. It was a larger, domed structure with five tunnels radiating outward in a star pattern.

"Which one do we take?" Grayle asked.

Sarah's mind flashed back to the Topkapi blueprints from last night. The location of the circled cross hovered somewhere outside the Palace walls, like a footnote at the bottom of the map. *What if it wasn't a footnote? What if it actually showed us where we needed to go?* It was the best lead they had. Their only lead in fact.

"That one," she said, pointing at the shaft to the right.

They eased into the basin. Sarah held her laptop bag over her head. She sucked in a breath as the cold, putrid water inched up to her chest. They waded across and hoisted themselves into the far tunnel. It was tighter than the one they had just left. Stooping low, they shuffled on, brushing cobwebs out of their path.

Sarah thought she heard voices over the sound of trickling water. She stopped and doused the fireball.

"What is it?" Grayle whispered.

"Shhh," she hushed, warning them not to make a sound.

Sarah cast her Auralex senses outward like a net.

"Romans," she finally said, detecting six Folklorian auras in pursuit. "They've reached the basin. I don't think they know which tunnel we're in," she added, thankful she'd extinguished the fireball in time.

Her relief was cut short.

Shouts echoed from the shaft. Sarah felt the emotions of the six Romans switch from confusion to surprise. She heard punches being thrown, bodies being tossed, men crying out until their voices were silenced.

"What happened?" Grayle whispered.

Pause.

Sarah stretched her senses. More auras had joined the fray—Outlander auras.

"Crossers," she said. "Five of them."

She heard angry shouts, then five clear words: "Split up and find them."

A flashlight beam cut the darkness.

"They're coming this way. Go!"

They continued on in the dark, hurrying down one shaft after the next, trying to put distance between them and the Crusaders. There was no way to keep their movements a secret. Every splashing footfall, every rasping breath echoed down the tunnel. Sarah heard rats squeaking and was sure a spider had made its way down her shirt. She wanted to scream, but suppressed her freak out to a full body shake down.

After another ten minutes, Sarah knew they were lost. She had no clue which direction they were going, no clue which direction they *had* to go. Which tunnel took them to the Odin symbol? Which one led back outside? It was impossible to tell without a compass or the sun to re-orient themselves. Just when she thought they were doomed to roam the cisterns for eternity, Sarah heard squawking ahead.

She conjured a new fireball.

Two crows sat perched on a pile of crumbling bricks to her right.

Nazan stared at the black birds. "How in blazes did *those* get down here?"

Grayle cleared his throat. "Dunno. But maybe they can show us the way out."

One of the crows squawked and flapped his wings.

Grayle didn't seem surprised to see them. If anything, he looked relieved.

"There's no way birds ever go underground—not even crows," Sarah said. "The only ones who *might* belong to Odin."

Grayle's mouth opened and closed. It didn't take an Auralex to read he was hiding something.

She glared at him. "Is there something you're not telling me?"

Chapter 34

Grayle swallowed. In the flickering light of the fireball, he could see the flare of suspicion in Sarah's eyes. He was usually able to think of a lie to get him out of trouble, but not this time. This time he didn't know what to say.

"You're kidding me!" Sarah spat. "You've been in contact with Odin? For how long?"

"We met in Midgard."

"Midgard!" The fireball snuffed out. Grayle heard Sarah's footsteps splashing toward him. She grabbed him by the collar and pushed him hard against the cistern wall. Cold, wet slime seeped through his shirt.

"You've been holding out on me for *that* long?" The sting in Sarah's words was clear.

He fumbled for the right thing to say. "He told me—"

"Do you realize how dangerous it is getting involved with the gods?" she cut in.

"For crying out loud—he's no Hel."

"Oh my gods. You don't know what you're doing."

"Hey…everything alright back there?" Nazan called out. "I'm kind of in the dark over here."

The crows squawked their agreement.

"Yeah, you and me both," Sarah mumbled under her breath. She released her grip. "We're coming." Her footsteps splash away. Muttering the incantation, another fireball materialized.

"Sarah…I'm sorry," Grayle called after her.

"Let's get out of here," she said without looking back, "then we'll figure out what to do next."

"What's he sorry for?" Nazan asked. "And why does he keep calling you *Sarah*? Who's Sarah?"

Crap.

"What are you talking about? There's no Sarah," Grayle said, trying to brush her comment off as nonsense.

"You called her Sarah twice—just now and when you told her to follow us down the ladder."

Grayle's mind raced, thinking of some way to argue with her. For the second time in five minutes, he drew a blank.

He saw the angry glint in Sarah's eyes.

Nazan stumbled back a step. "Wait a second. Y-you're Sarah F-Finn, the renegade witch," Nazan stammered. "A warrant for your arrest was circulated last night."

Grayle wasn't sure if he heard her right. "Warrant? What warrant? What is *she* talking about?"

"Nothing," Sarah said.

"Please…let me go," Nazan pleaded. "I won't tell anyone who you are or where—"

"Sorry. Can't do that." Sarah's hand shot out, pinching the girl's neck. "Rauco-balan." Nazan went into spasms as an electric current surged through her body. With a strangled groan, her eyes rolled back and she collapsed at Sarah's feet.

Grayle rushed forward. "What'd you do that for?"

"Had to. Hamza and the Ottomans betrayed us. Can't take a chance she was in on it."

"Why would they betray us? They needed our help."

Sarah bit her lip. As far as poker faces went, she didn't have one.

"The warrant…is that what this is about?" Grayle pressed.

She threw her arms in the air. "Fine. I found out the Coven put a warrant out for our arrest. The Ottomans, or Hamza at least, gave us up in exchange for the reward money."

"*Our* arrest? They want me too?"

"Not exactly. They put a bounty on your head…dead or alive."

"Oh this is great, just great. When were you planning on telling me?"

"After we got the runestone."

Grayle stared at Nazan's body slumped against the cistern wall.

"She'll be okay," Sarah reassured him. "She'll come to in a few minutes. Let's go."

Grayle didn't budge. "She might be okay, but *I'm* not. You're keeping things from me again! How am I supposed to trust you if you don't tell me everything?"

"*I* don't tell you everything—" She stopped and took a deep breath. "You're the one who's conspiring with gods behind my back."

"You make it sound like we're hatching some kind of sinister plot. Odin wants to help us find the Eye, that's why he sent his crows."

Cawww. Cawww.

"Do you know how hard it is for a witch to trust a Hexhunter—our mortal enemy?" Sarah said, shaking her head. "Can you even fathom what that must be like?"

"Excuse me for being something I didn't know I was until yesterday." He couldn't keep the anger from his voice. "Have I given you any other reason not to trust me?"

She didn't answer. Part of him didn't want her to. He was afraid she'd say yes.

Sarah glowered at him. "Fine. So we're even."

"This isn't about keeping score. It's about *really* trusting each other."

Rushing footsteps from a nearby corridor alerted them it was time to go.

"This isn't the time," Sarah hissed. "We have to keep moving."

Grayle bent down to pick up Nazan.

"No. Don't," Sarah whispered, already making her way down the next tunnel.

"We can't just leave her here. The Crossers'll get her."

"The Crossers don't want her…they want us. Trust me. She'll be okay."

Grayle stood there, looking down at the girl. Another casualty in their quest for the Eye. *How many others are going to get hurt before all this is over?*

He turned to the crows. "Lead the way, guys."

The birds flew ahead, appearing and disappearing in the darkness as if the black was swallowing and spitting them out over and over again. Grayle and Sarah followed their guides through the passageways, bypassing several side tunnels that would have otherwise made them second guess their route and slow them down. This went on for another ten minutes until they emerged from a pool of shadows and reached a wall of large sandstone bricks. Slivers of daylight seeped between the crumbling mortar.

"This must be it," Grayle said.

Huginn and Muninn perched on a nearby beam. *Cawww. Cawww.*

Sarah let her fireball fizzle out. She took a deep breath. "You might want to get out of the way," she warned.

Grayle shuffled aside as a surge of blue energy engulfed Sarah's arms. Stepping toward the wall, she released her magic with a single word: "Vanya!"

The pulse spell blasted away at the bricks. When the dust settled, there was a four-foot hole in the wall.

Shielding his eyes, Grayle climbed out into the daylight first. They had emerged underneath the Topkapi Palace, along the walls that had protected the palace for centuries. The sea crashed against sharp rocks far below to his right. But the remnant of a roughly hewn stairway was chiseled into the side of the wall like an ancient scar. It was narrow and only led one way—down.

"Watch yourself," Grayle cautioned. Loose gravel kicked out from under his shoe. The stairs were weathered and brittle, making their descent all the more treacherous. One false move, one errant step, and they could slip and tumble to the rocky shoreline below.

"You think anyone's been here over the years?"

Sarah slipped, almost losing her balance. "I don't think so. This side of Constantinople would have been too steep to mount an attack. And I doubt recreational hikers would've come here either. How much farther is it?"

Huginn and Muninn glided clockwise, landing on a short, flat outcropping thirty feet below.

"A little more."

They hurried down as fast as the terrain would allow. Their fingers clawed at the stones, steadying their descent. Grayle glanced up, keeping a nervous eye on the opening where they came from. He expected Crossers to come pouring out at any moment. If that happened, there wouldn't be a place left for him and Sarah to hide. They'd be caught, at the mercy of Sebastian Caine and whatever he had planned for them.

"Is this it?" Grayle asked, reaching the outcropping. They were at the base of Constantinople's walls, where the finely cut sandstone met the rough, natural granite on which the Topkapi Palace was built.

Huginn or Muninn, Grayle couldn't tell which, flapped his wings and let out a shrill screech.

"I'll take that as a yes."

Sarah got to work inspecting the wall. The earth dropped off around them. If there was an entrance to a tomb, it had to be here.

"What exactly are we looking for?" Grayle asked.

"A lever of some kind. Maybe a keyhole. A doorknob would be nice, too."

Sarah placed her hands on the sandstone. "Tana!"

With a rumble, the outline of a door appeared.

"That wasn't so hard," Grayle said.

She turned and glared at him.

"Right. Sorry." He had a way of jinxing things when he said stuff like that.

She rolled her eyes and turned back to the wall. "Edro."

The rock face shuddered, loosening centuries of dirt and erosion from its frame.

"Edro!" she repeated more forcefully.

Larger chunks of stone broke free from the door's surface. A small, hand-carved rectangle appeared, including what looked like the outline of a keyhole.

Need you must the emeralds three,
To use as the doorway's key.

"You're up," Sarah said, backing away.

Grayle retrieved the dagger from his waistband and pulled the knife from its scabbard. The polished blade gleamed in the sunlight. He tried not to think about what it had done in its long past—how many people it had killed.

He jammed it into the opening. The slot was too wide for the dagger's blade to fit properly. There was too much room on either side, like using the wrong bit size on a screw, and not enough leverage to turn it. Grayle flipped the dagger around, handle first. He carefully slid it inside the notch. It fit perfectly. He adjusted his grip on the blade, preparing to give it a good push into the keyhole.

A mix of green stone and liquid red.

Liquid red.

Blood?

Grayle clenched his jaw. *It would be just like Halfdan, or whoever made this lock, to make it painful to open.* He already felt the blade cutting into his skin. *This is going to hurt.*

Caine's helicopter suddenly came roaring overhead.

Huginn and Muninn screeched and scrambled into the air.

The helicopter swooped over the hillside and banked sharp to the left. It hovered sideways, coming toward them. The whir and hurricane-like winds of its rotors was deafening.

"Get us in, Grayle! Get us in!" Sarah shouted.

Grayle looked over his shoulder. The chopper's cabin door slid open. A Crusader sat there, aiming a machine gun. Before he could fire, two black streaks shot into the aircraft. Rather than fly to safety, Huginn and Muninn attacked the helicopter as if it were a predator invading their territory. The chopper buffeted as the pilot tried to fight off the crows and control the machine at the same time. Grayle had experienced a crow attack firsthand—the slicing talons, the pecking beaks, the confusion of flapping and slapping wings. It wasn't a good experience.

Bullets sprayed into the bricks over his head.

"What are you waiting for? Open the damn door!" Sarah screamed. "Ga'la!" The shadow of her shield grew to cover them.

Grayle grit his teeth as the dagger sliced into his flesh. His palms and fingers oozed blood, first one drop, then a slow dribble of deep crimson. It trickled down the blade, onto the handle, then into the keyhole. Like a sponge, the surrounding stone soaked in his blood, working its way into the minute cracks and crevices around the keyhole.

The wall shuddered. Grayle felt rather than heard something disengage inside the ancient door. Old gears, hidden in the masonry, creaked to life.

Grayle pushed, straining every muscle. More dirt loosened. The door gave way, unleashing centuries of trapped air. Beyond, framed by cobwebs and carpeted in dust, was the Tomb of Serpents.

Chapter 35

Sarah slipped into the tomb behind Grayle, keeping her shield poised between them and the strafing bullets. Once inside, she shrunk the shield and heaved on the door.

"Why do they have to make these things so heavy?" she shouted over the deafening helicopter rotors. "Grayle. Help me."

Grayle tucked the dagger into the waistband of his cargo pants and added his shoulder to the door. Together they pushed as hard as they could but couldn't close it all the way.

The chopper's downdraft billowed dust and debris like a mini-tornado through the crack. Sarah saw the tail end of a rope drop onto the outcrop.

They're coming.

She grabbed Grayle's unbloodied hand. "Mind where you step," she said. The terrain was uneven and strewn with debris. "The clue stone warned us about traps."

She pulled him deeper into the tomb. The ceiling rose fifty feet above them, supported by massive pillars, two of which had toppled over, lying on the stone floor like fallen redwoods. Carvings ran up each support, scenes depicting battles between armies and monsters. Sarah recognized gryphons, double-headed eagles, centaurs and a dragon, struggling against heroic warriors in armor, each frozen in terrifying detail. The pictures spiralled upward, disappearing into the shadows of the darkened ceiling.

The sound of grinding stone scraped behind them. The door was being pushed open again.

"Quick—hide!" Sarah scrambled over toppled statues and hid behind the farthest fallen pillar. Grayle followed, flattening on the floor beside her. The cuts along his palm and fingers were bleeding badly.

"Here." Sarah took out the pashmina Nazan had given her and tied it around his hand. Grayle winced as she tightened the knot. "This'll have to do for now," she said and peered through a crack in the pillar.

Five men in black commando uniforms rushed into the tomb, securing the entrance. Mussels lumbered in after them. Caine entered a moment later, covering his mouth with a handkerchief.

The billionaire did a quick scan. "Find them," he ordered.

Sarah watched the lead Crusader, the Alpha, bring two fingers to his eyes, then point them left and right. The squad fanned out, sidestepping deeper into the tomb. The Alpha stalked down the middle. The other four split, sneaking around from the far left and right sides.

A classic pincer maneuver.

Each Crosser hit squad had an Alpha and nine operatives. With five operatives possibly lost inside the cistern, these five were it.

Still five too many, Sarah thought.

"Where can we go?" Grayle whispered.

Flashlight beams attached to the Crossers' M16s played over the room.

Other than the entrance, Sarah couldn't see another way in or out. What might have once been a staircase on the opposite side of the tomb had caved in centuries ago. For the time being, the bulk of the toppled statues and stone pillars sheltered them from view. But not for long. It was only a matter of time before their position was revealed.

"Dunno," she whispered back. "But be ready to move."

Sarah heard him jostle about, shaking his legs as if he were kicking off bedsheets.

"What are you doing?" she hissed.

"My feet. They're caught in something."

Sarah reached down to help loosen whatever had tangled around him. In the beams of the Crusader's flashlights, she could make out something draped along the floor. Sarah held up the transparent substance. It felt rubbery between her fingers with a slight bumpy texture.

"It almost looks like snakeskin," she said.

"No way. It's too big to be a—"

Sssss.

The hairs on Sarah's neck stood on end.

Dust fell from the ceiling, fluttering to the floor like snowflakes.

Sssss.

Grayle groaned. "I have a bad feeling about this."

Heart pumping, Sarah peered through the crack. Caine and his mercenaries had heard the hissing too. They stopped, their weapons trained at the ceiling. One of the columns teetered, then another several yards away. Was something crawling above their heads, hidden in the shadows?

Sssss.

Sarah couldn't pinpoint the source of the hissing, but it was growing louder. The very air seemed to vibrate around her. Then, as quickly as it came, the sound stopped.

Everything became still.

Sarah heard the rasp of her own breathing, the thud of her heartbeat drumming in her chest.

Without warning, a scaly tail lashed out from the shadows. Like a noose, it snared one of the Crusaders around the neck and yanked him screaming into the darkness.

His comrades retaliated. Machine gun muzzles flashed. Shell casings clinked onto the tomb floor. Bullets sparked off stone, ricocheting in every direction.

Crack! Crack! Crack!

The Alpha raised his fist. The Crossers ceased fire—and waited.

A machine gun fell from the ceiling. It clattered somewhere in the darkness, absent its owner.

"Delta One, secure the entrance," the Alpha shouted. "Beta team, continue searching for—"

A giant serpent corkscrewed down the nearest pillar. In one quick motion, it snatched the Alpha in its jaws before he could finish his orders. Bones crunched, arms and legs flailed like a rag doll, until the soldier's body dangled lifeless in the monster's mouth. With one terrible toss, the snake threw its head back, swallowing the mercenary whole.

Caine drew his gun. Mussels did the same.

For a second time, the tomb erupted in gunfire.

The serpent uncoiled and whipped its tail fiercely from side to side. Its scales were like plate armor, but even it couldn't withstand twenty-first century weapons for long. It slammed into nearby pillars, tossing debris across the tomb. Rock chips juddered from the ceiling. If they weren't careful, they'd bring the entire roof down on top of them.

Sarah gawked in wide-eyed terror as the beast slithered in their direction. She pushed Grayle aside and rolled out of the serpent's path. Mottled skin of browns, yellows, and greens flashed in front of her, each scale clearly visible on its tube-like body.

The snake whipped around, surprised at the movement of new prey. It lashed out its tail. Sarah rolled to her feet and swerved to the side in one lithe motion. Grayle wasn't so lucky. The serpent's tail caught him square in the chest, launching him across the tomb.

The viper reared like a cobra, exposing its yellow-scaled hood. Fangs the size of sabres flashed in its gaping mouth. Before it struck, another hail of bullets peppered it from behind. Hissing angrily, the snake twisted back towards Caine.

Without knowing it, the billionaire and his henchmen had probably just saved Sarah's life.

She picked her way to where Grayle lay sprawled and dazed among the rubble. A nasty cut bled from his cheek.

"You okay?" she asked. His arm felt limp as she helped him up.

He clutched his ribs and nodded. "We need to get out of here."

She couldn't agree more.

Sarah guided him farther from the combat zone to the far side of the tomb. She scooped up the first Crosser's abandoned M16 and detached the flashlight mounted on its muzzle. It was still switched on.

They kept low, zig-zagging their way from points of cover. The serpent had kicked up so much dust a thick haze clung to the ground. Flashlight beams from the remaining mercenaries' machine guns created a chaotic lightshow.

Reaching the far wall, Sarah noticed the stone surface was pockmarked with holes large enough for the serpent to squeeze through.

Is this how it gets from one part of the Tomb to the other?

At the moment, Sarah didn't care. She aimed the flashlight into one of the holes. It slanted downwards farther than the beam could reach.

"It's our only way out of here," she whispered.

Sarah laced her fingers, helping Grayle up into the hole.

He wriggled in feet first. Sarah handed him her bag and shield. "You sure about this?" he asked.

"You want to stay here?"

The answer came in the form of another loud hiss and bullets spattering into the stone next to them.

Grayle let go, vanishing into the darkness.

Sarah stepped back, ran, and dived in headfirst after him.

Chapter 36

Why won't this thing die!

Caine loaded another clip into his Beretta. He fired at the creature until it clicked empty.

Rather than cowering away, the serpent turned and accelerated toward him.

Caine drew back. There was nowhere to hide.

Mussels arrived at his side, unloading his Herstel into the viper's face. Enraged, the serpent thrashed wildly and reversed course. Caine knew it was only a temporary retreat.

"Orders, sir?" asked Beta One—the new Alpha. His voice was shaking.

"Stand your ground, soldier." Caine had forgotten the man's name.

"But we're outmatched, sir!"

"I said stand your ground! We need those kids."

He'd lost sight of Finn and Rowen during the battle. Were they hiding? Had the serpent gotten them? He thought he'd seen movement in the dust cloud a minute earlier, two silhouettes dashing to the far side of the tomb.

"I didn't sign up for this," Beta One shouted. "I'm taking Delta One and getting out of here." He spoke into his radio, "Bell Two-Four-Niner. We need an evac. Now!" He backpedalled, laying down cover fire as he and Delta One inched toward the tomb door.

Static responded. "No LZ. Repeat, no LZ."

LZ = Landing Zone.

"We're coming out anyway!"

Mussels grabbed the mercenary before he got any farther.

"Let go of me!" Beta One shouted.

The bodyguard said nothing. He reached down and unpinned three grenades strapped to the Crusader's vest.

Beta One became hysterical. "What are you doing?" He fumbled for the grenades. They would go off any second.

Mussels lifted the man by the belt and tossed him to where the serpent lurked in the shadows. The beast welcomed the easy prey. It lunged, snatching Beta One in one horrible bite. The soldier barely managed a scream before disappearing down the creature's throat.

Mussels threw his body in front of Caine as the grenades went off.

The explosion came like a wet squelch. Pieces of shredded snake spattered everywhere, smothering the surrounding stone in a layer of fleshy red. Headless, the serpent's body writhed in its death throes. It crashed mindlessly into pillars, cracking the supports and sending debris flying everywhere. Unable to sustain the ceiling's weight any longer, the damaged columns exploded in a thousand pieces.

Mussels shielded his employer from the stone shrapnel. A piece of collapsing pillar the size of a Volkswagon crashed inches from where they stood.

"Aller!" Mussels yelled, pushing Caine toward the exit.

More sections of the ceiling came thundering down around them.

"The whole place is caving in!" warned the last Crusader over the din of falling rocks. "We need to evacuate!"

Even with the serpent gone, Caine knew it was too dangerous to stay.

"Retreat!" he shouted, letting Mussels half-push, half-carry him to the exit. He knew what leaving now would mean. The witch and Hexhunter would get the runestone. He'd have to take it from them another way.

* * *

The Operative expertly hovered the Bell 212 over the rocky outcropping. He'd flown Blackhawks in Somalia and Afghanistan, completing routine reconnaissance and combat missions under heavy gunfire.

He'd never been attacked by crows though.

His helmet had protected his face from the feathered onslaught, but his bare arms were crisscrossed with talon marks. The birds had retreated once the witch and Hexhunter entered the tomb. Leftover feathers still fluttered in the cockpit.

The stone door opened below.

Mussels appeared, carrying Caine with one arm and pulling the door closed with the other. A single mercenary slipped out before it shut completely.

That's it? Only three?

Nine had entered, including the witch and Hexhunter. What became of *them*?

The Operative angled the chopper closer, bringing the rope ladder within arm's reach of the three men. Once they were safely aboard, he pulled the throttle back and to the right. The helicopter juddered. The upward force of the rotors pushed the chopper into the air, and the tomb's entrance shrank away.

"Circle around. I want to see if they make it out," Caine ordered, settling into the co-pilot's chair. His clothes were covered in blood and what looked like bits of flesh.

What the heck happened in there?

"Sir, the Turkish Air Force has ordered us to land at once," said the Operative, mimicking the original pilot's voice. "They're sending aircraft to intercept." Thanks to the helmet and darkened visor, the billionaire didn't suspect his pilot had been replaced.

"Blasted military." Caine slammed his fist against the helicopter's plastic window. "Take us to the nearest airfield," he said. "We'll have to come back another way."

The Operative hid a smile as he swung the chopper away from the Topkapi Palace. One to two hours would pass before Caine could return to the area.

The witch and Hexhunter won't have to worry about him anymore. Provided the two were still alive.

His smile faded.

And if they were alive, they were completely on their own now.

Chapter 37

Grayle's backside felt like tenderized meat. It was like being inside a slide at a swimming pool, only a lot rougher. Skin scraped off his back and elbows. He knocked his head against the tunnel's ceiling too. He kept low after that, wishing—praying—the slide would soon come to a happy ending. Seconds later, it spat him out six feet above the ground. He landed hard on his side. Sarah's bag and mini-shield shot out after him.

Grayle sank his teeth into his lip, trying to ignore the pain that wracked his body. He opened his eyes. He had to blink several times before realizing he hadn't gone blind.

A moment later, he heard something else come sliding out.

Oof!

"Sarah?" Grayle whispered hoarsely. He got to his knees, groping about himself, careful not to bump into anything in the dark. "Sarah?"

She groaned. "Yeah."

Grayle slid his hands in wide arcs until his fingers touched her boot.

"Naur-galad."

A small flame pierced the darkness, magically flickering in Sarah's palm.

She had scratches on her face and her clothes were ripped, but she seemed otherwise unhurt. Grayle imagined he looked the same. His cargo pants were torn at the knees and the shawl bandaging his hand was damp with blood.

"Where are we?" Sarah croaked.

A quick scan of the cavern confirmed they were alone.

"Deeper underground," Grayle figured.

They fell silent, trying to hear signs of the battle somewhere above.

Nothing, but that didn't mean they were out of danger.

"We better get moving," Sarah suggested. She winced as she stood. "It won't take the serpent long to search these tunnels."

Grayle swallowed. "You think it's still alive?" He got up and handed her her shield and laptop bag. She slung each over a different shoulder.

"Pretty sure it'll take more than bullets to kill it," she said. "Look on the bright side, I don't think we'll have to worry about Caine following us."

"Your *bright side* needs brightening. Have you given any thought how *we're* going to get out of here?"

"One problem at a time. Let's focus on getting the runestone first."

She held the fireball higher.

They were in another cavern. The walls were crude, bare stone with only one exit—a narrow tunnel carved through solid rock.

"I guess we go this way," she said.

They went in single file. The tunnel twisted sharply, creating blind turns with no way of knowing what might be lurking around the next corner. Apart from their own breathing and the crunch of their footsteps, there was no sound either. It was as if the blackness was wiping out sound as well as vision.

After a hundred yards, they came to a junction. The tunnel branched off in a trio of different directions.

"Which one do we take?" Grayle asked. His voice echoed down all three shafts.

"Not sure," Sarah said.

Without Huginn or Muninn to guide them, they were on their own.

"Didn't Halfdan believe in leaving breadcrumbs?" he said.

"He probably didn't want to make it easy for anyone to find the stone."

"Well score one for the Viking."

"Which way do *you* think we should go?" Sarah asked.

Grayle noticed the subtle anticipation in her voice. "Since when do you ask me for directions?"

She shrugged. "Just wondering what your instincts are telling you."

"You mean my Hexhunter instincts?"

Sarah mentioned how Hexhunters in the past were drawn to magic, how they used their instincts to hunt down witches. Grayle refused to believe he was descended from people who were capable of murder. Still, whatever his feelings were about Hexhunters and their sordid past, he couldn't deny a strong urge to go right.

"This one," he said.

"See? That wasn't so hard."

Shield strapped to her back, Sarah entered first. The new shaft was large enough to walk side by side.

"So what does Odin want from you anyway?" she asked, brushing aside a low hanging cobweb.

Grayle knew it was only a matter of time before she brought up the subject again. She'd keep pressing him until she had her answers, but he was in no mood for another round of bickering. "He wants to help us find the Eye." He thought she'd be relieved knowing the king of the Viking gods was on their side.

"I don't trust him," she said instead.

"Why shouldn't we trust him of all people?"

"Because he's not *people*, Grayle. He's a god—obsessed with knowing the future. He gave up his eye in order to take a drink from Mimir's Well, all so he could get a glimpse of the future. That kind of obsession doesn't simply disappear."

"He told me the gods don't have the power they once had. That's why he needs me to retrieve the Eye—keep it out of Hel's hands and prevent her from freeing Loki."

Sarah stayed quiet for a long moment. "That might be the case," she said finally. "But I still think he wants the Eye for himself."

Could she be right? Does Odin have an ulterior motive for helping us?

Grayle thought back to their last meeting, the look on Odin's face when he asked him for something in return for his help. *Was it anger? Contempt? A glimpse of his true nature?* Grayle didn't want to believe the All-Father was deceiving them. They had so many enemies; he wanted to hold onto the one ally he thought he could trust.

"Well, Odin told me he doesn't want his eye back."

"Right. And you always tell the truth?"

"You're one to talk." He was about to remind her that withholding information was just as bad as lying when a low rumbling came from somewhere deep inside the earth.

Grayle's breath hitched. "What was that?"

Sarah's eyes went wide.

Dirt suddenly rained down in clods, falling on their heads and into their shirts.

The cavern they were in shuddered. Then the walls began closing in.

"Go!" Grayle shouted, pushing Sarah forward.

Pebbles clinked off her shield. "The tunnel's collapsing!" she yelled.

As one, they bounded down the shaft. The rumble exploded to a roar.

They shuffled sideways, racing through the shrinking space, knocking against the walls like pinballs. Dust blinded Grayle's eyes and clogged his lungs. He felt the weight of rock and soil crushing down on him. It was horrible, like being buried alive.

Sarah doused the fireball, replacing it with the faint blue glow of her hands. She ran ahead, palms open, arms stretched out to either side.

"Vanya!"

As if hitting a pause button, the tunnel stopped its relentless effort to turn them into pancakes.

But only for a moment.

The blue glow sputtered. Sarah was losing power.

Grayle thought he could feel rocks tumbling at his heels. Just when he expected to be crushed, they emerged into a larger cavern. Grayle dropped to his knees, hacking, gasping, desperate to breathe. A plume of dust and earthy air shot from the tunnel as it grinded shut behind them.

Chapter 38

"Naur-galad."

Sarah levitated a new fireball from her palm. Behind her, the tunnel's black maw re-opened with a rumble, ready to crush its next victims.

"Must have been one of the traps the clue stone warned us about," she said.

Grayle stood and brushed off his backside. "Ya think, Captain Obvious?"

Sarah ignored his sarcasm. She hovered the fireball higher. The light only reached a few yards ahead. She strained to make the flame grow brighter, but couldn't. Her magical reserves were depleting. Too much magic expended in a short period of time. She was growing tired, becoming more unfocused with every minute.

"We need to keep going," she said, unsure whether the words were meant for Grayle or to convince her that's what they needed to do.

Another cavern gaped in front of them, dark and foreboding. They crept forward. Sarah carefully negotiated each step, scanning the ground for anything that could set off another trap. Stalactites hung above them like ice-cream cones shoved into the ceiling. The floor was riddled with broken boulders as if someone had come along and smashed them with a sledgehammer. Several empty sets of clothes and chainmail lay among them. Looking closer, Sarah saw the bleached remains of human bones: a rib cage, several skulls, and multiple femurs.

"What happened here?" Grayle whispered.

Sarah fixed her gaze on the mangled skeletons strewn across the cave floor like a forgotten graveyard. "A battle of some kind, I think." A sword and an axe head glinted in the firelight. "Whatever this is, we're on the right track. I bet you anything these were Halfdan's men."

"How can you be sure?" Grayle asked.

"Look at the clothing." She pointed to a group of skeletons wearing leaf mail and woollen tunics, the same style they'd seen in Midgard. "This is good…very good."

Grayle frowned. "You kidding me? How can this be good!?"

"Don't you see? The more dead Vikings we find, the more we can be sure no one's been in the tomb since Halfdan sealed it. Which means there's a good chance the runestone is still here."

"Also means that whoever, or *what*ever, they were fighting could still be in here too. You think the serpent did this?"

Sarah shrugged. "Not sure."

They continued on, hopping past the fallen rubble and scattered bones, careful not to disturb them. More boulders the size of ox carts lay partly smashed along the length of the cavern. Some skeletons lay crushed underneath.

No sooner had they reached the middle of the cavern when Sarah heard tinkling sounds like wind chimes. The stalactites above them wobbled back and forth like dangling spears. The first stalactite dislodged before Sarah could yell, "Watch out!" They sprang in opposite directions as the stone icicle crashed between them. The ground shook and dust plumed on impact.

"Head for the walls!" Grayle shouted.

Two more stalactites came crashing down, but exhaustion slowed Sarah's reflexes. One of them grazed her shoulder, knocking her against the cavern's edge. The fireball winked out. Rocks splattered in the darkness. The cave filled with falling debris.

Sarah shut her eyes and clung to the wall like Velcro. It wasn't until the noise died down and the crack of tumbling rock dissipated that she re-ignited another flame. It sputtered to life, only weaker and dim.

"I'm really starting to hate caves, Sarah," Grayle shouted from the opposite side of the chamber. "*Really* starting to hate them."

She coughed, waving dust from her face. "You and me both."

"Do we keep going?" Grayle called out.

"I don't think we have a choice," she said reluctantly.

As the dust settled, she could make out another opening on the far side of the cavern. It was an arch made of brick and mortar. "There…to your left. A way out."

They shimmied close to the safety of the wall and out of the path of falling debris. Sarah moved as if she were walking barefoot on glass.

Reaching the archway, she saw it was large, with a radius of nearly twenty feet. Ornate carvings covered its curved frame. It looked Roman, predating the Vikings by at least five hundred years. Sarah figured the chamber could be much older than that.

"Um…Sarah." Grayle pointed to an Odin Cross cut into the arch's keystone. "Looks like we're on the right track after all."

She smiled. "Our first breadcrumb. And look at this." She focused the fireball's light on three rows of runes etched into the stone to their right—long, deep cuts, hastily scored into the aging brick.

Sarah took out her laptop, surprised it had survived the cistern waters and cave-in. The screen's brightness blinded her. Accessing the futhark rune database, she entered the script. The translation scrolled across the screen a moment later.

> *Go no further.*
> *Seek thy knowledge elsewhere.*
> *You will only find death here.*

"Cheerful," Grayle muttered.

"I think Halfdan wrote these," Sarah said. "A warning to strike fear into anyone who made it this far."

"Like a giant snake, cave-ins, and almost being speared by stalactites didn't do it already?"

Sarah closed the laptop and tucked it back into her bag. "Let's hope those were the last of his traps." She went to stand up but stumbled sideways. The fireball flickered.

Grayle shot to his feet. "You okay?"

"I'm fine," she said, closing her eyes and taking a deep breath.

She wasn't fine. Her hair stuck to her skin, and she felt sweat trickling down her temple.

"You don't look fine."

The fireball fizzled again.

"You need to rest," Grayle said, taking her arm and placing it over his shoulder. Sarah leaned against him, clinging tightly to his shirt.

She shook her head. "No. I'll be...I'll be..." She drew in a short, quick breath. Her knees wobbled, and she collapsed, hanging limp in his arms. Sarah felt her eyes rolling back, and then everything went black.

Chapter 39

"You!" Brenna stomped toward her stalker, sword firmly gripped in one hand. "You're dumber than I thought, coming alone and presenting yourself for a beating."

Lothar Ericson backpedalled. "Wait. Stop!" The prince raised both palms in surrender. "I came to help you."

Brenna grabbed him by his tunic, twisting the thick fabric in her hand. "You could've helped me by telling Malin the truth—that I was kidnapped. But you decided to do as you were told...like the obedient dog you are."

Lothar stood his ground. "I am no one's dog." He broke Brenna's hold and pushed her away.

Hrafn came swooping down like a winged fury before Brenna could retaliate. The bird swiped at the prince's face with his talons.

Lothar tripped, falling onto the cobblestones. "Stop! Please!" he pleaded, swatting his hands in an attempt to fend off the crow. "Whatever I said wouldn't have made a difference."

"What do you mean?"

"Get this blasted bird off me and I'll tell you!"

"Hrafn. Haetta!"

The crow ceased his attack and flew onto her shoulder.

Bad prince, he cawed.

Brenna couldn't agree more. "Okay," she said, looming over Lothar. "Talk."

The prince stayed where he was, afraid any sudden movement would send the bird dive bombing again. "The decision that you *weren't* kidnapped was made even before you came into the Onem's lab."

"Who decided that?"

"Onem and Malin."

"Why?"

"Why do you think?" He was out of breath and his cheeks were flushed. "Have you given any thought what would happen if others found out Hel was behind your kidnapping?"

"Um, they'd find out the truth. Because she *did* kidnap me."

Lothar got up. He straightened his tunic and gave Hrafn a wary glare. "You don't get it. The safety of the Folklore Kingdoms is dependent on the people's faith in our magic. Imagine what would happen if House Ericson, House Bloodaxe, or House Hardrada lost that faith. What would happen if they learned we were no longer of use, that someone like Hel could just stroll into their walled city and snatch souls whenever it pleased her? What do you think would happen then?"

Brenna knew exactly what would happen. Vikings, especially the lords from the ruling Houses, had always been suspicious of magickers. They saw a witch and warlock's magic as a threat to their power. The only reason magickers were tolerated was because they provided protection against enemies like Frost Giants, dark elves, and trolls. Lose that trust, and tolerance would quickly turn to hostility.

"Even if I had sided with you," Lothar went on, "it wouldn't have made a difference. Malin will stop at nothing to preserve the reputation of magickers, even if it means calling you a liar or—"

"—Sarah a renegade," Brenna hated to admit it, but what he said made sense. She hadn't considered Midgard politics in all of this. Being next in line to be Midgard's king when he turned sixteen, Lothar had a more intimate understanding of how to keep the ruling Houses at peace.

She felt her anger cool. Maybe she wasn't going to punch him after all…not yet anyway.

"So what are you doing here?" Lothar asked, scanning the wilderness around them. "Are you looking for where the wall was breached?"

Brenna sheathed her sword and nodded. "There has to be a gap somewhere, some place Hel and the traitor exploited. I was told this could be a likely spot."

Lothar sneered. "Who told you?"

"Someone I trust," Brenna replied with an edge to her voice warning him to stop prying.

The prince got the hint. "What were you planning to do once you found the breach?"

"Find evidence of tampering, I guess. The wall's defenses were specifically designed to repel magic from Helheim and the other Nine Realms. There are only a handful of people in Midgard who can tamper with the wall's defenses. It had to be someone with magical abilities."

"That rules out ninety-five percent of the people here," Lothar noted.

Brenna nodded. "And of the remaining five percent, who had something to gain by helping the Death Queen?"

The prince thought for a moment before saying, "We may not find *that* out until it's too late."

"That's what I figured too. So instead of looking for a motive, I thought it may be easier to find the breach itself. Magic leaves a trace—an echo. It works like a fingerprint, unique to the magicker. Find the breach, and we may uncover the traitor. But I'm not sure I can separate one magical signature from the next. There's something here though, infiltrating the defense's magic. Can you feel it?"

"I felt it from farther down the slope. Where is it coming from?"

Brenna examined the Pillar of Halvor. The natural monolith jutted fifty feet straight from the mountainside. "Look." She pointed to a section where erosion had broken off chunks of granite, leaving a reddish rock exposed underneath. Brenna may have done poorly in her elixir and incineration classes, but she did well in geology. She recognized the rock instantly.

"It's iron," Lothar confirmed.

The metal, even in its raw form, had weakened the wall's magical defenses.

How many sections have been compromised this way? she wondered.

There was more. Odd horizontal markings gouged the Pillar where the chunks had cracked off. The granite's natural grain was vertical, which meant the horizontal markings were manmade.

Brenna stepped closer to get a better look. The weakness from being disconnected from the ambient energy intensified. She grew dizzy again and backed away.

"You smell that?" Lothar asked.

Brenna sniffed, only now catching a whiff of something pungent, almost toxic, in the air. "It almost smells like brimstone. Someone magical *did* pass through here."

Lothar's face turned white. "And the only one powerful enough to do that—"

"Is Hel," Brenna finished. "This *must* be the place where she got in."

The prince surveyed the area nervously. "I-If the iron is affecting us f-from this distance," he stammered, "wouldn't it have weakened Hel too?"

Brenna shrugged. "She's far more powerful than any of us. She might have been able to push through, with the help of the traitor." She examined the rusty iron deposits. "The iron's interference probably scattered the magical fingerprint by now. It'll be impossible to get an accurate reading. Something the traitor was surely counting on."

"So if we can't find out who helped her get in, what do we do?"

"We tell someone," Brenna decided, her frustrations growing. She'd found the spot where Hel crossed into Midgard but couldn't get the proof she needed. "That's about all we *can* do for now. C'mon. Let's head back."

They turned and started their trek down the ramparts. Hrafn flew from Brenna's shoulder, off to stretch his wings.

"Maybe we're going about this the wrong way," Brenna said. She was unwilling to let it go, especially when they were getting so close. "Instead of focusing on the traitor, we should be looking at Hel. Why did she need to get into Midgard?"

"To get the Hexhunter," Lothar said matter-of-factly.

"If that were the case, why didn't she get him while he was locked up in the Great Hall?"

The prince thought for a moment, then said, "Hel didn't know where the next runestone was either. She needed the information as much as we did and knew the Hex would want some kind of payment in exchange. What better way than showing up with a meal?"

"Yeah, but Hel could've taken any girl or boy as an offering. She chose me on purpose. Why?"

"I don't know. In order to stay close to the Hexhunter?"

That was the only thing that made sense.

"Okay, so it comes back to her wanting Grayle. She wanted to capture him—alive. Remember? She trapped him in ice in Baldersted."

"Then why did Frost Giants try to kill us on the mountain yesterday?"

Brenna frowned. "Wait…what?"

"It happened after you were kidnapped…on our way to Baldersted," Lothar explained. "Three Jotun were waiting for us shortly after our journey through the bifrost. They loosed an avalanche, almost killing us." He drew himself a little straighter. "We would have been killed if it wasn't for my quick thinking."

"I didn't know you were ambushed." Now that Brenna thought about it, she had no idea what Hel did while she assumed her form. "Someone must have told the giants you were coming, which means someone—" She didn't get a chance to finish.

Hrafn suddenly cried out from the sky. *Danger.*

Brenna froze. "Stop," she said.

Hide, the crow screeched.

Brenna grabbed Lothar's sleeve and jerked him aside just as an arrow came shooting from a stand of trees to her left. The arrow missed by inches, disappearing over the wall and into Idun Falls.

"Get down!" she shouted. Brenna hurled herself forward, rolling to a stop behind the wall's crenelling. Another arrow sparked off the stone where Lothar found cover next to her.

"Did you tell anyone where you were going? Were you followed?" Brenna shouted.

Lothar cringed behind the battlements. "No!" he whimpered. "I swear."

Bjorn warned her someone might want to silence her, if only to keep the traitor's identity a secret. Brenna had drawn too much attention to herself. Now they were pinned down, faomrs away from help. And the gods only knew how many assassins had come to kill them.

Chapter 40

Sarah's eyelids felt like they were made of stone. She forced them open. Everything was pitch black. No up, down, left or right. Just darkness. If it weren't for the cold rock beneath her, Sarah would have thought she was floating in a sea of blackness.

She sat up and rubbed her arms, willing the friction to warm them. She winced, touching the lump where the Roman guard had whacked her. She was about to conjure a fireball when she realized she didn't need to. A dim glow emanated from the tunnel opening ahead.

"Where's that light coming from?" she asked.

No answer. Only then did she realize she was alone.

"Grayle?" she whispered.

Nothing.

"Grayle." A little louder.

Where is he?

She stood up slowly, looking to see if Grayle was somewhere on the ground nearby. Maybe he'd fallen asleep too?

"Sarah."

She jumped at the sound of her name.

"Sarah."

It wasn't Grayle. The voice sounded familiar though. Sarah spun, searching for where it was coming from.

"Sweetheart, it's me."

A gray mist shimmered in front of her, its edges blurry, undefined. The figure was hard to make out, fading in and out like a lost signal. It slowly took shape into a slim woman in her thirties with long black hair and pale blue eyes.

"Mum!" Sarah rushed toward her. The wake of her movement brushed against the mist, distorting the spectre's image. Sarah stopped. "Mum?" Tears gathered in her eyes. "W-where are you? What's going on?"

"I'm in the underworld, sweetheart. In Helheim."

Sarah's mouth went dry. "Helheim? What are you doing there?"

"There's no time to explain." Her mother's spirit glided closer. "Hel has only granted me a few moments. Any longer and my spirit may waste away."

Sarah's breathing became shallow. "Mum, how did you—"

The spectre lifted a hand. "As I said, I don't have much time. Hel has sent me to make a deal with you."

"Deal? W-what deal?"

"The Death Queen wants you to retrieve the remaining pieces of Mimir's Stone…for her."

"For *her*. Are you nuts?"

"Hear me out. If you manage to do this…" Her mother paused.

Sarah couldn't read the expression on the spirit's face. Was it regret? Uncertainty? Shame?

"If you manage to do this," she continued, "Hel will restore me to life."

Sarah stood there, unable to process what she was saying. "Is that even possible?"

"She assured me it was."

This can't be real, Sarah thought. *Hel's gotten the better of me too many times.* She took a step back. "How do I know you're really my Mum, and not some trick?"

The spectre looked hurt, then seemed to understand the reasoning behind Sarah's mistrust. "I know it's hard to believe, and there's so much at stake, but if there's a chance…"

The proposal hung there between them, tempting and unbelievable.

Sarah still wasn't buying it. "My real mother wouldn't ask me to do this."

"And if things were different, I wouldn't ask. But Hel is not to be trifled with. What the Death Queen wants, she usually gets."

Sarah huffed. "I've encountered Hel twice now, and I'm still here. I can handle her."

"Don't be a fool," the spirit scolded. "Hel has only been toying with you until now. If you don't accept her terms, she threatened to kill you and reunite us in the underworld."

Sarah kept quiet. What if her mother was right, that Hel had the power to bring her back to life? Was it a chance Sarah was willing to take? Not so much for her own sake, but to get her mother's tormented soul out of Helheim?

"I'll have to think about it," she said. "We don't even have a runestone."

There was hopefulness in the spectre's expression. "Not yet," her mother said, "but you're strong and resourceful. And you're with a Hexhunter." She swallowed, visibly shaken. "Be careful around him, Sarah. Hexhunters are not to be trusted."

"Grayle's different." The words came like a reflex. She had gotten used to defending him.

The spectre's form withered.

"Mum?"

"I must return. Hel is calling me back to her. Be careful, sweetheart."

"Mum!" There was still so much Sarah wanted to say. She stepped toward the vanishing figure. "Don't go! I miss you. I—"

The ghost was already gone.

Sarah stood there, staring into the darkness.

Did that just happen? It seemed too unreal. Her mother had been dead for years, and now her spirit decided to show up—with a proposal from Hel? Find the runestones and hand them over in exchange for *maybe* restoring her back to life? *And what kind of life would that be? As soon as Hel gets the runestones, she'll use them to find the Eye of Odin. That'll start Ragnarok. Not much of a happy ending if—*

A hand touched her shoulder. Sarah let out a yelp.

"Relax. It's me," Grayle said.

Sarah swung around and slapped his arm. "What are you doing sneaking up on me like that?" she hissed.

"Ow. Take it easy. I was scouting ahead and found something. Who were you talking to?"

"Myself," she lied. Sarah turned away before Grayle saw she was on the verge of tears. How was she going to explain her mother's visit to him?

Easy. I'm not.

She took a deep breath and waited for her pulse to slow. "What did you find?"

His grin looked eerie in the cavern's glow. "Come and see." He turned and passed under the arch.

"Where are you going?" Sarah whispered nervously.

"You'll see."

She wasn't in the mood for games.

"How are you feeling?" Grayle asked.

"Better." Her magic levels had replenished somewhat after the power nap, but far from full strength.

Grayle stopped after thirty yards. Sarah peered over his shoulder.

The tunnel opened onto a yawning chasm. A ray of daylight cut through the darkness from an opening somewhere high above, shining like a spotlight onto a black stone in the middle of the wide expanse.

The runestone.

The proportions were different; this one was smaller than the fragment they found in the Vancouver Museum, but the dark obsidian with its greenish hues was unmistakable. Even from where she stood, Sarah could make out runes etched onto its smooth surface.

"You found it," she breathed.

The marker rested on a long, solitary pillar jutting from the middle of the chasm. Three rings of stone slabs, equally spaced apart, floated around it. The slabs were almost five feet in diameter and made of limestone. They rotated in opposite directions and at different speeds, orbiting the central pillar like the dials of a giant clock.

Sarah swallowed. "We're going to have to cross on those, aren't we?"

Grayle nodded, his gaze fixed on the runestone.

"Well, I think we can do it," Sarah said, trying to sound upbeat. "The stones are close enough together for us to jump across."

"It's not going to be that easy," Grayle said grimly. He knelt down on the chasm's edge. A floating stone glided by within arm's reach. He stretched and put his hand on it. The instant his fingers made contact, the stone dropped out of sight.

Sarah stared at the empty space where the stone had been a second ago.

"I'm a Hexhunter," Grayle said, standing up again. "Whatever magic is at work here, it won't allow me to get across. Maybe you'll have better luck. Touch one and see."

Sarah squatted on her heels. As she reached out her fingers and brushed the stone's rough surface, it also fell away like a lead weight. She shook her head. "Why put floating stones around the runestone if there's no way to get across?"

"There has to be a way, we just haven't found it yet," Grayle reasoned. "The rings remind me of a combination lock. We just need to find the right combination."

Looking closer, Sarah couldn't believe what she was seeing. Roughly hewn runes glowed pale green on the surface of each slab. "You're right. It *is* a combination lock. Each stone has a rune."

"Really?"

Sarah nodded. "I can see their auras. Some are more faint than others, but they're definitely there—a different one on each stone."

"So we need to spell something out, like a password?"

"Looks like it."

Grayle got on all fours again and brought his cheek down to ground level.

"What are you doing?" Sarah asked.

"Scanning the top of each stone."

"For what?"

"I'm hoping whoever crossed here last left a trail of some kind, showing us which stones to jump onto."

Not a bad idea, Sarah thought, *but wishful thinking.* "After hundreds of years, any sign of Halfdan's crossing would probably have been erased," she said. "There might be another way though."

Sarah sat cross-legged in the dirt and took out her laptop. She displayed the Futhark alphabet, all twenty-four characters. She spent precious time inputting the letters from all three rings, creating a virtual representation of the stone slabs and their corresponding rune symbols. When she finished, they could see every possible combination of three letter Norse words, from *bro* meaning a bridge to *ung* for young—almost sixty combinations in all.

Sarah's optimism deflated. "It's no use. We might as well be guessing."

"What about the center column?" Grayle pointed back to the pillar around which the stones floated.

"What about it?"

"Does it have a rune?"

Sarah squinted, trying to make out whatever was etched on the platform's surface. "It looks like the Odin symbol."

"If we add that to the letter combinations, does it spell anything else?"

Sarah shook her head. "The Odin symbol is just that—a symbol—not an actual letter in the Norse alphabet."

"Then why is it there? Every rune or symbol we've discovered so far has meant something or told us where to go next, like the runes in the Hagia Sophia and the circled cross on the Ottoman blueprints."

"Oh my gods." Sarah put her face in her palms and shook her head. "How could I be so stupid?"

"What's wrong?"

"Where else have we seen the Odin symbol?" she asked.

"On the Ottoman map."

"No…more recently?"

"Above the ar—" Grayle began.

Sarah clapped the laptop shut and was on her feet before he finished answering. She rushed down the tunnel they'd just come from. Grayle close behind. Together they backtracked to the arch. In the dim gloom, Sarah made out the circled-cross crowning the brickwork. The runes warning them of danger were off to the lower right.

"Touch the runes, Grayle," she said, her optimism returning.

He did.

Sure enough, his contact caused the runes to glow. But instead of revealing new script, three letters glowed brighter than the rest.

Sti.

"What does it mean?"

Sarah typed the letters into the translator.

She smiled. "It means *path*."

Chapter 41

Path.

Of course the password would be something obvious.

If it weren't for the deadly traps he and Sarah had already encountered, Grayle would have guessed Halfdan had a sense of humor. He didn't feel like laughing though. The mystery behind why magical runes glowed whenever he touched them wasn't funny. It was frustrating.

"How am I doing this, Sarah?" he asked, keeping his hand on the carved runes. "If I'm a Hexhunter, I'm not supposed to have any magic. So how are they glowing?"

"I can't be sure, but I think we're...I think we're connected somehow."

Grayle raised an eyebrow. "We're what?"

Sarah bit her bottom lip. "Let me try something."

She took a few steps back, widening the distance between them. As she did, the runes on the archway started to fade like someone was lowering a dimmer switch.

Grayle stared in disbelief. This whole time he thought he may be someone special, possessing a kind of unearthly power, when all along it was Sarah. No, it was a combination of them both.

He swallowed. "We *are* connected. How did you know?"

She shook her head, obviously as confused as he was. "I didn't. But I suspected something was up when I saw the runes on the floating stones." Her face turned grim. "We should be repelling one another, like two negative sides of a magnet. But that's not happening." The runes re-appeared as she returned to his side. "Turns out we're more like the positive and negative sides of a battery, generating a new power when we're together."

"But we're supposed to be sworn enemies—not you and me, but witches and Hexhunters."

"I know," Sarah agreed. "But there's evidence to suggest other- wise."

"What evidence?"

"C'mon. Let's head back. I'll tell you."

They hurried down the tunnel, returning to the floating stones.

"Every clue or trap we've encountered so far has been designed to help or kill a witch or Hexhunter *if* they were on their own," Sarah began. "The shrinking cave, your added touch making runes glow, me being able to see the runes on the floating stones. Who knows, maybe the blood needed to open the tomb door had to be the blood of a Hexhunter."

"We're not going back to test that theory," Grayle said quickly.

"I wasn't planning to," Sarah said. "But together we've been able to survive. *Together* we've been able to beat the odds."

They reached the chasm and gazed at the runestone. It sat there, taunting them. So close and yet unreachable.

"You know what the chances are for an Auralex and Hexhunter to find each other and then team up?"

"One in a million?" Grayle guessed.

"Try astronomical. That's what makes these traps so ingenious."

If her theory was correct, it only raised more questions. "If the chances are so astronomical, it means something more might be at work here."

"It could be our fate or destiny," Sarah suggested. "Maybe even luck?"

Grayle raised his bloodied hand. The cuts under the makeshift bandage still stung. "Strange...I don't feel lucky."

Sarah let out a long breath. "I know...I'm not a big believer in luck either. It's better than the alternative though."

"Which is?"

Her blue eyes hardened. "That someone's planned all this. That someone is pulling our strings like puppets in a marionette show."

People pulling strings was nothing new for Grayle. Sly and Irma Zito, the warden at Gloomshroud, maybe even the woman in the feathered cloak from his dreams—all had been puppetmasters in his life at some point.

"Puppet show or not," he said, "we still need the runestone. How do we get across?"

Sarah pursed her lips. "We have to cross together, just like we did when we used the bifrost."

Grayle wasn't finding the connection. "What does the bifrost have to do with anything?"

"Traveling by bifrost is a magical gateway," Sarah explained. "By all accounts, you shouldn't have been able to pass through, but—"

"But I was holding on to you and we made it," Grayle cut in.

"Exactly. People's auras have a flow, a unity that can either be fragmented or linked. Magickers can combine their powers while in physical contact with one another—I had to do that with Lothar in order to take down the magic disguising the Hex's house in Baldersted, and then again later to help him conjure a bifrost. Maybe something like that is happening here…with us."

"But you said I don't have an aura."

"You don't…not one I can see anyway. But when I put my arms around you at bifrost bridge, something worked. I didn't even think of it at the time, but my aura must have surrounded you. If it didn't, the bifrost's magic wouldn't have worked on you."

Grayle stared at the floating slabs. "So what you're saying is that in order for us to get the runestone, not only do we have to jump onto the floating stones in the right order, but we're going to have to hold onto one another while doing it?"

"Yup."

Suddenly the surface of each slab looked cramped and uninviting.

* * *

An Auralex and Hexhunter having to work together to retrieve an artifact? Sarah had never heard of anything like it before. Could it explain Grayle's abilities and why he didn't show all the characteristics of a Hexhunter? Was he a tamer, more civilized, low-fat version of a Hexhunter compared to those in the past?

"Let's test my theory before we go jumping ahead," Sarah cautioned. She grabbed Grayle's hand, and together they knelt on the chasm's edge. "Here it comes…the stone with the *S* rune." She stretched out with her other hand. The stone resisted as she pushed down on it.

It worked. Her theory was correct.

Halfdan created puzzles and traps only a witch and Hexhunter working together could crack.

Not just a witch, Sarah reminded herself. *An Auralex.*

Only an Auralex could have seen the runes glowing on the floating stones. Only an Auralex could meld auras with another person. And somehow, maybe only an Auralex reacted differently to a Hexhunter.

An Auralex must…

The words were etched on the runestone from the Vancouver Museum.

An Auralex must…must what? That was a good question.

"You ready?" Grayle asked, pulling Sarah from her thoughts.

She nodded. "As ready as I'll ever be."

She placed her hand in his open palm and focused her senses. She forced her aura to surround them. Grayle's darkness resisted. Like a cold wave, it pushed her away.

"Relax," she told him. "And trust me."

Sarah tried again. Rather than imposing her aura onto Grayle, she focused on casting it wider, surrounding him entirely like a protective shield. She felt it close around him. They were ready.

The floating stone circled back toward them. The *S* rune glimmered in the low light. Suddenly the stone surface seemed cramped and impossible. They let it go by.

"We jump *on* the count of three," she stressed, recalling their clumsy plunge into the bifrost two days earlier. Instead of a nice, smooth entrance into the bifrost, Grayle stumbled. It made for a gut-wrenching ride through the bridge.

"You ready?" she asked.

Grayle nodded, preparing himself.

"One…"

The stone was coming again. She could see it. Instead of another glow in the darkness, it took form—a flat slab, no more than five feet wide.

"Two…"

Grayle's hand twitched in hers.

"Three."

They jumped in unison. The stone sank under their combined weight, but stayed afloat. Sarah wobbled before correcting her balance. With their feet firmly planted, the invisible current carried them around the chasm.

Grayle let out a relieved whistle. "This isn't going to be so hard after all. Whoa!" The second ring of stones began orbiting the pillar faster, as if someone put it into another gear.

Sarah groaned. "You just had to say something, didn't you?"

The increased speed complicated matters. Now they were jumping from one moving object onto another moving target.

Sarah craned her neck, searching for the *T* slab. "Here comes the next one. We're going to have to jump earlier—"

"—to compensate for the added speed, I know," Grayle said.

Her muscles tensed as the stone soared closer.

"One…two…three!"

They jumped, this time landing awkwardly. The slab teetered, and Grayle's feet slipped away. He tumbled off, managing to grab onto the stone's edge at the last second.

It all happened so fast it took Sarah a second to realize their connection had been broken.

The stone plummeted.

The shock of freefalling and the wind whooshing in Sarah's ears sent her screaming. She dropped to one knee and snatched Grayle's wrist. The shift in weight threatened to tip the slab over. Sarah refused to let him go. She hooked her feet on the opposite edge. Looking past his shoulder, Sarah could make out the faint outlines of stalagmites jutting from the chasm floor. Two impaled skeletons hung there like skewered fish on a spear.

Deep empty eye sockets stared up at her; jaws gaped in a silent, frozen howl.

Their connection re-established, the stone began to climb again.

"Give me your other hand," Sarah yelled.

Grayle reached. She clasped his forearm and pulled him up.

She wrapped her arms around him, partly out of pure elation and partly to keep her anchored to the floating stone. She couldn't stop the frantic thumping in her chest. They stayed on their knees hugging one another, not daring to move until the slab rose and resumed its place among the other circling stones.

Sarah felt Grayle's muscles stiffen. He broke their embrace.

The final ring circled even faster now. The runes were a blur. Only by matching her eyes to the slab's speed could she make out the final letter: *I*

How are we going to reach the runestone now?

Chapter 42

Grayle stared wide-eyed as the final ring whipped around at warp speed. Okay, maybe not warp speed, but too fast to confidently stick a landing. He knew the sheer momentum at which the stones were spinning would buck them off. It would be like jumping on a high-speed treadmill, sideways, and trying not fall on your face. Except in this case, falling on your face meant plunging down a hundred foot chasm.

"We don't land on it," Sarah said out-of-the-blue.

"What?"

"The last stone…we don't land on it, we jump off it—use it like a stepping stone—a spring board."

"And land on the pillar?" Grayle said, his voice shaking.

Sarah pursed her lips and nodded. "It's the only way."

She'd been right about the other stuff—Istanbul being the capital of the east, the Hagia Sophia, the importance of the Odin Cross on the Ottoman map—why not this? It seemed her theory about them being connected was right too. If that was the case, it meant the chance of their meeting wasn't a coincidence. Someone, or something, had to be behind all this. It was planned.

And if this is planned, what was the endgame?

The thought was unsettling.

"Grayle. Focus!" Sarah snapped. "Are you ready?"

He nodded and took a deep breath.

"It's that one," Sarah said, pointing at one of the slabs zipping by.

Grayle tracked the stone's trajectory, but lost sight of it once it entered the darkness on the far side of the chasm.

"We jump, land on one foot, then push off again," Sarah reminded him.

"Tell me when…on three."

They crouched together, tensing their muscles and mustering their courage. The pillar's width looked inviting after the cramped, unsteady stones.

Her hand squeezed his. "One…"

Grayle glanced at the runestone. It was calling to him.

"Two…"

He didn't remember feeling the same attraction to the stone in the Vancouver Museum, so why now? Had his exposure to magic and Folklore awakened something inside him?

"Three!"

They jumped in perfect synchronicity. For a fraction of a second, Grayle felt relief as his foot made contact with the stone. Then his world upended. The slab's momentum catapulted him into the air like an out-of-control gymnast. His hand wrenched away from Sarah's. Not knowing which way was up or down, he expected to freefall to his death. Then his shoulder hit rough gravel. The breath was smashed out of him. He felt the impact take the skin off his shoulder. It left him dazed.

Sarah had landed next to him.

Groaning, they rolled on their backs and found one another's hands again.

"You okay?" Grayle asked, helping Sarah to her feet.

She nodded. A new scrape on her temple glistened with fresh blood, adding to the bruises and fat lip she already had.

Behind them, the floating stones slowly returned to their peaceful, winding current as if no one had trespassed.

You are close now, Hexhunter.

Grayle turned and stared at the runestone. It called to him, beckoning him to come closer. He stepped toward it. Like the stone in the Vancouver Museum, the runes began to glow a translucent green the nearer he came. More letters bled to the surface, filling the empty spaces.

Sarah took out her smartphone and snapped pictures.

Grayle tensed. The last time they were this close to one of the fragments, Hel appeared and almost killed them.

"What do the runes say?" he asked.

Sarah put her phone away and retrieved the laptop from her bag. Her eyebrows knit together as the translation scrolled across the screen.

Her eyes went wide. "Oh my gods!"

"What? What is it?"

Take it, Hexhunter, the voices chorused inside his mind. *It is yours for the taking.*

"C'mon," Grayle said. "What are we waiting for?"

He went to grab the stone.

Sarah's hand shot out, stopping him. "Wait. Don't. Something isn't right."

"Is it another trap?"

"No…and that's what worries me. This seems too easy. There has to be a catch."

Now, Hexhunter. Before it's too late.

Grayle clenched his teeth. The urge to take the stone was overwhelming. His body moved automatically.

"Grayle! No!"

Too late.

He reached out and seized the runestone with both hands. A jolt ripped through his body. His arms vibrated, unable to let go of the fragment. He was vaguely aware of Sarah gasping and stepping away. Then the cavern spun, wheeling around him as a million threads of light cascaded across his mind. Embedded within each were thousands of images blending together like a colorful symphony.

The voices chorused louder than ever: *Find me, Hexhunter. Find me.*

His mind reeled, trying to work out what was happening. He tried to steady himself, not even sure if he was standing anymore. "Who are you? What is this? What's happening?"

They didn't answer.

A rush of jumbled images overwhelmed his senses. The scenes passed in rapid succession, flashing long enough for him to see what they were but not long enough to get a clear understanding of what they meant. He could make out a bronze helmet, an old castle nestled next to a dark blue lake, and Sarah, her eyes red from crying.

The scenes disappeared, and Grayle found himself back among the light strands. What did the images mean? None of them revealed a hint to his own burning questions, what he really wanted to know: *Where did I come from? Who are my parents?*

No sooner had his thoughts turned to his family when new fibres rushed by in a twisted helix pattern. The images slowed, and he found himself transported into what looked like a bedroom. The still scene sharpened and surrounded him. Grayle stood before a four-poster bed. A woman lay pale and sweating on its mattress. Sheets and pillows were pulled around her in a twisted mass of fabric. A man leaned over her, holding her hand.

"What is this?" Grayle asked.

This is your birth, the voices explained.

"Those are…"

Your parents.

Grayle stared at the man frozen in suspended animation. His father, really? He was taller than Grayle expected, but they shared the same gray eyes and unkempt hair. He wore a dark business suit. The first two buttons of his collared shirt were undone.

A round woman with a thick, fleshy face kneeled at the foot of the bed. *A midwife,* Grayle guessed. Two servants in white aprons stood by her side.

Behind his father, crooked as a question mark, stood a familiar figure. Onem, Midgard's Loremaster.

What is he doing here?

The old warlock looked much as he did when Grayle saw him two days ago, striding in front of a grand bonfire at the All-Thing in Midgard.

In a darkened alcove to his right were three young girls, maybe nine or ten years old. They were identical to one another except for their hair color. One was blonde, the other a ginger, and the third dark-haired. They held onto the dark robe of another figure hidden in the shadows. An oversized cowl obscured her face, but Grayle recognized her at once.

The woman with the feathered cloak.

She and Onem had been here at the beginning.

As if pressing a play button, the scene began to unfold around Grayle.

"Stay with me, m'lady. You must push," yelled the midwife. The woman reached for another towel, urgently trying to stop his mother's bleeding,

Frightened servants stood idly by as his mother wailed in pain. "She's been in labor for hours," Grayle overheard one of them say. "Something is wrong." They both glanced nervously at the woman in the feathered cloak.

The triplets let go of her robe and came forward.

"Do not fear for your safety…" the blonde one said first, trying to alleviate the tension in the room.

"…or that of your lady," the redheaded girl added.

"No harm will come to any of you," the dark-haired one assured.

Before the servants could respond, Grayle's mother screamed and clutched her bed sheets.

"That's it, m'lady. Push."

His mother bore down and did as the midwife instructed. She screamed in agony, then fell into her pillows, gasping for air.

The silence was broken by a baby's cry.

"It's a boy!" the midwife announced.

Grayle looked on, unable to speak.

The midwife cut the umbilical cord and wrapped him—the baby him—in a powder blue blanket.

"Well," his father said, turning toward Onem. "What of the child?"

The Loremaster's green cloak swished as he approached the bedside. Leaning over, he inspected the newborn with a long, guarded gaze. He extended a gnarled hand, hovering his bony fingers over the baby. He closed his eyes. The wrinkles creasing his forehead deepened. "It is as we feared. He is a Hexhunter."

His father recoiled. "Get rid of it."

"But m'lord…" the midwife protested.

"I don't care how, just do it before the agents arrive."

As if on cue, Grayle heard a car screeching to a halt outside. Doors opened and slammed shut. Heels clacked on pavement, crossing the street.

"They're coming," the blonde triplet warned.

"If it is to happen…" added the redhead.

"…it needs to happen now," finished the dark-haired girl.

The midwife turned to Grayle's mother. "Surely, m'lady, you cannot—"

There was a loud bang. Someone was trying to kick in the house door downstairs.

"You heard my husband," his mother said. Her soft eyes didn't match the harshness of her words. Bottom lip quivering, she added, "He is an abomination. Get it out of my sight." Then she turned away and sank into her pillows, sobbing.

Grayle spoke in barely a whisper. "Mom. Dad." The words were foreign, dying on his lips. "They…they didn't want me?"

No, the voices answered coldly. *You must have suspected that the reason no one came looking for you is because they didn't want to.*

Grayle had, but he never wanted to believe it. Hearing someone else say the words suddenly made it real. They cut deeper than he expected.

With a final crash, the agents broke through the door below. A voice shouted orders. Rushing feet came tramping up the stairs.

The woman in the feathered cloak stepped into the light. "Give him to me," she ordered, holding out her arms. "I will see to his end. Quickly now."

The midwife, her cheeks moist and red, hesitated at first, then handed over the infant.

Onem swept across the chamber. "Are you mad? You must kill it *now*, before—"

The robed figure shot him a look, stopping him mid-sentence.

The three triplets came forward and tugged on the warlock's sleeve.

"Let her take him," the blonde girl said.

"It is the best for everyone," said the redhead.

"His fate is sealed," said the dark-haired girl.

There was a thump at the bedroom door. "Open up!" a gruff voice shouted. "We know you're in there."

Grayle watched as the woman folded the baby him in her feathered cloak.

His father sidled next to her. "Make sure the deed is done," he said under his breath.

The woman's head nodded under her cowl.

Bang. Bang. Bang. The bedroom door shook on its hinges.

The triplets hurried over and clung to the woman's robe. In a flash, their bodies burst into a murder of crows. Wings flapped in a chaotic black swirl until they vanished out the open window.

The chamber froze just as men in black trench coats broke into the bedroom.

Anger coursed through Grayle's veins like ice. Just like that, the hopes and dreams he'd been clinging to for years were shattered. There would be no happy ending to his story, no happy family reunion. His mother and father weren't waiting for their missing boy. No brother or sister would be running to welcome him home. Instead, they had wanted him dead.

All is not lost, Hexhunter, the voices soothed. *Find me, and together we can punish those responsible for abandoning you.*

That was the last thing Grayle heard as the bedroom and voices spiraled, growing fainter until they faded altogether. He was back among the light threads, feeling colder and more alone than ever.

Chapter 43

S arah gawked as Grayle lit up like a Christmas tree.

What in Helheim was happening?

An aura enveloped him as soon as he touched the runestone. For the first time, Sarah could see a spectral veil of silvery blue. His eyes ignited, irises sizzling with the same brilliant color. She was mesmerized by the power consuming him.

"Grayle?" she said gently.

No reaction.

"Grayle!"

He stood there, his face vacant.

Every fear she harbored about the nature of his powers came roaring to the surface. Was his connection to the runestone merely a fluke, or was this the beginning of something else? Was his body becoming normal—able to produce and project an aura? Worse, was some kind of latent Hexhunter power taking over?

She reached out and touched his arm.

As if coming out of a trance, Grayle's connection to the stone wavered.

"You okay?" Sarah asked. "What happened?"

He muttered something under his breath and removed his hold on the stone. He looked shaken. Whatever happened had obviously been traumatic.

Sarah didn't press him. She turned to the runestone and tapped it, testing to see whether it would affect her.

Nothing.

"What are you doing?" Grayle asked. His words came out breathless, as if he had just run a marathon.

Sarah opened her bag. "I'm taking the stone." Exactly what she was going to do with it afterwards remained uncertain. Could she really give it to Hel in exchange for her mother's resurrection? Would she jeopardize Folklore and the entire world to do it?

I'll figure that out later.

She hovered her palm an inch over the artifact. "Cidinn." The runestone shrank to the size of a baseball. She carefully lifted it off the pedestal and tucked it into her bag.

A cracking sound reverberated throughout the cavern.

Grayle's eyes saucered. "What did you do?"

"I don't kn—"

Waterspouts suddenly exploded from the chasm walls, shooting water like bursting fire hydrants. Ten, twenty, fifty spouts erupted.

"The chasm must have been rigged to flood if someone took the stone," Sarah shouted above the roar of gushing water.

Was this Halfdan's final trap? His last attempt to kill whoever dared enter the tomb and steal the runestone?

Sarah didn't want to find out. She rushed to the edge of the pillar. Grayle staggered after her. They could already see a dark murkiness inching up the pillar. Water swirled like an overflowing toilet bowl, rising higher and higher toward them. Bones and debris were caught in the current, a lot more than the two skeletons Sarah had seen impaled on the stalagmites minutes earlier.

Rats swam in the current too, their little legs desperately fighting to stay above the surface.

There's no way I'm swimming in that.

Sarah took Grayle's hand and was about to jump onto the first floating stone when all three rings dropped away, splashing into the rising water. With a great rumble of falling rock, the cavern opening through which they'd first entered also sealed itself shut.

Grayle cursed beside her. "How are we going to get out of here now?"

Sarah's phone rang before she could answer him. *The Good, The Bad, and The Ugly* barely registered above the noise of rushing water. Sarah fumbled for the device. "Grigs? Grigs, is that you?"

The reception was poor. All she heard was static and a few garbled words.

"Sarah. Where…tarnashin'…? Romans chasin'…goin' to sail…for…"

"Grigs, we're trapped! We need help. I'm turning on my locater app. Did you get that? I'm turning on my locater app."

No response, just more static. Then the connection went dead. They were too far underground.

Sarah swiped the screen and turned on the app. At this point, she didn't care who could detect her signal. Escaping the tomb was priority number one, even if it meant revealing her location to Malin.

By the time she put her phone away, the rising water had submerged the pillar. It was freezing, creeping up Sarah's feet, then her knees.

The powerful undertow swept both their feet out from under them, sending her and Grayle spinning around the cavern. Sarah screamed, her shouts drowned out by the deafening torrent filling the chamber. She caught a glimpse of Grayle bobbing in the water ahead. She tried not to lose him. For a second she was sure she had. Then she saw him through a break of whitewater. He was drawing away from her. She had to reach him. Her legs kicked, her arms thrashed. Her breath ripped from her lungs. But she made herself breathe deeper, move faster. A rat clung to her hair. Sarah freaked. She thrashed about wildly, trying to get the vermin off. She dove under the surface, forcing the critter to bail. When she no longer felt the rodent's tiny claws digging into her hair, Sarah re-emerged.

I have to get out of the water, she told herself.

She pushed a floating rib cage out of the way. Two more stow-away rats clung to it like a life raft.

That gave her an idea.

Sarah scrambled to stay afloat while tugging the shield from her bag. It had saved her in the past, and now it may do so again. Placing it's curved side on the surface, Sarah chanted her growth spell: "Ga'la!" The shield quadrupled in size. She pulled herself awkwardly on top of it.

Getting on her knees, Sarah scanned the flooding cavern for Grayle. She saw him twenty feet away, fighting to stay above water. Sarah shifted her weight, able to angle the shield as she rode the current. She reached him in a matter of seconds. Luckily Grayle saw her coming. He grabbed for the shield's edge. His hand slipped off, and he disappeared under the water.

"Grayle!" she shouted.

He broke through the surface behind her, gasping for air.

Sarah circled the chasm once more, using her knees to veer the shield back in Grayle's direction.

"Take my hand!" she yelled as she drew closer.

He swam and thrust out his hand, straining to reach her. Their fingers hooked together first, then locked into a solid grasp. Sarah pulled him aboard and wrapped her arms around his neck.

"Are you alright?" she shouted.

He coughed, but she felt his head nodding against her shoulder.

The daylight seeping from the hole in the cavern's ceiling grinded shut. Sarah and Grayle were left in darkness, surfing blindly on the water's spinning current.

"Naur-galad." Sarah conjured another fireball in her palm. She willed the flame to float above their heads, climbing higher until it hung just below the stone roof.

The rising water pushed them closer to it. What would happen when the cavern filled completely? No room to swim, no air to breathe. They'd drown.

"There has to be a way out of here," she said. The icy water and adrenaline rush cleared her thinking. The hole that had filtered daylight into the cavern may be covered, but it was still there. And if there was a mechanism that sprang to close it, there had to be one that opened it again.

"There!" Grayle pointed to where the opening had been—a rough, circular depression maybe four feet wide. "How do we open it?"

"Look for a lever or switch."

They passed the depression once, twice, each time unable to spot anything that could unlock it. All the while, the cavern ceiling grew closer. It wasn't long before Sarah had to duck to keep from banging her head against low hanging stalactites. By the third lap around, she spied a rectangle chiselled into the stone. "Grayle! A keyhole." It was an exact copy of the keyhole they found at the entrance to the Tomb of Serpents. "Hurry! Take out the dagger."

Grayle reached back and pulled the emerald knife from his waistband.

"I'll try and grab on somewhere to hold us in place," Sarah said. "Long enough for you to use it."

They went around the chasm again. They stayed low. The ceiling pressed down on them, getting too close for comfort. Like a pinball, the shield banged into the stalactites, their calcium tips already submerged in the water. The impacts deflected them off course, steering them wide of the keyhole.

"Push off the stalactites if they get too close!" she told Grayle.

The strategy worked. Using the stalactites, they were able to guide their direction in a controlled approached to the doorway. Sarah managed to hang on to the outer edge of the depression. The rush of the spinning current and rising water made it harder to stay aboard the shield. Little by little, water began spilling in. Sarah couldn't hang on for much longer. They were sinking.

"Grab hold of something, Grayle! We have to get off."

He did, snatching a tiny stalagmite jutting next to the keyhole.

Sarah reached down with her free hand. "Cidinn!" With a blue flash, the shield shrunk from under them and disappeared in the twisting, murky water.

Sarah was sorry to see it go. It had helped her on so many occasions.

It won't help me if we die here, she thought.

Grayle was already using his teeth to remove the soiled pashmina from his hand. Cuts gouged his palm where the dagger had sliced it earlier. He wrapped the material around the dagger's blade. Sarah couldn't blame him. Blood still oozed from his cuts, not as bad as before, but enough to leave red streaks dribbling down his arm. No need to lacerate the other one. Grayle pressed his bloodied palm against the keyhole and, at the same time, twisted the dagger's handle in the lock.

Nothing happened.

Grayle shifted his hand and tried turning the dagger again.

It wouldn't budge.

"It's not working!"

Sarah stretched her neck. The water had reached her chin. Drowning rats squealed somewhere nearby. "What's wrong?" she asked.

"I don't know! I'm doing exactly what I did last time."

The fireball hissed and sizzled as the water came in contact with it.

How much time did they have left?

"Cut my hand," Sarah said. Her voice shivered, both from fear and the water's freezing temperature.

"What?"

"If we really are connected, maybe I need to sacrifice *my* blood to get us out."

It was also the only option they had left.

Grayle pulled the dagger from the keyhole and took her hand underwater.

He hesitated.

"Do it!" Sarah sputtered. Her head pressed against the cavern's ceiling. They only had seconds left.

She felt a cold sting as the dagger's blade sliced deep into her hand. She flinched. Dark crimson bloomed in the water. She reached up and pressed her hand around the keyhole. Grayle thrust the dagger's handle back into the keyhole. He turned it.

Still nothing.

The water crept over their noses and mouths. The fireball sizzled out. Everything went pitch black.

Sarah pushed her hand harder against the ceiling, as if that would make the blood seep into the stone any faster. She could feel Grayle desperately twisting his body, trying to wrench the lock open.

It was no use.

Maybe they weren't connected. Maybe she'd been wrong about the whole thing.

She couldn't hold her breath any longer. Her lungs were screaming for oxygen. She needed to breathe.

That's when she heard it.

The mechanisms opening the ceiling hatch rumbled, sounding like dull thuds underwater.

The pressure building in the flooded cavern suddenly released in one explosive force. A powerful flow sucked Sarah through the opening, shooting her out like a spouting geyser. The next thing she knew, she was airborne. The chasm's darkness switched to brilliant sunshine. Wind raced over her shoulders. The jettison upward gave way to gravity. She started falling.

Crap. This is going to hurt.

She prepared for a bone-shattering collision against the rocky shore. Thankfully, it never came.

Sarah plunged feet first into the Golden Horn, allowing the estuary's waters to embrace her. It felt warm and soothing compared to the murky chill inside the abyss. She opened her eyes. The salt water stung, but she needed to know where she was going. The water was surprisingly clear. Grayle was already swimming to the surface. She could just make out his silhouette and something else—something circular. Her shield. It must have ejected from the chasm with her.

Sarah kicked and snatched the shield on her way up. She broke the surface, coughing water still trapped in her lungs. She blinked rapidly, adjusting to the dazzling sunlight after spending so much time in the tomb. The ancient walls of Constantinople loomed high above her. Twisting in the water, she saw the *Drakkar* coming around the bend, chased by three Roman triremes.

Grayle had spotted the ship too. He waved his arms, trying to get the longship's attention.

Sarah did the same. "Here! Over here!" she shouted.

The Drakkar veered in their direction. A thick net jettisoned overboard. It trailed in the water, ready to snare them.

Sarah swam to Grayle's side. Without saying a word, they both reached out together and hooked an arm into the net's loopholes. The force almost tore Sarah's shoulder from her socket. Every ounce of her remaining strength went into holding on as the net slowly pulled her and Grayle aboard.

Chapter 44

Minutes went by since the last arrow ricocheted off the wall above Brenna's head. The break in the attack could mean one of two things: whoever was out there was waiting for them to reveal themselves, or their adversaries were slowly closing in on their position. Either way, the situation was bad. They couldn't stay waiting to be picked off or be surrounded.

"You need to do something!" Sarah shouted in Lothar's direction. "Throw a pulse spell or toss some fireballs!"

Bravery was not in the prince's vocabulary. He stayed put, curled in a ball and shaking like a leaf. Brenna would have to get them out of this herself.

With no help for faomrs and stuck so far from Midgard in the wilds that surrounded the Norse Folklore, the attackers must have thought the isolation was the perfect spot for their ambush. But it had its advantages—especially for a Dyr'talara.

Brenna was in her element. Apart from the wall, the wilderness was untouched by mankind's interference, strengthening her link to the ambient energy. She closed her eyes and forced herself to relax. She slowed her breathing, felt the pulse of her beating heart.

Then she turned her attention outward. Her pulse fell in rhythm with the beat of the forest. It came alive around her—the breeze, the smell of pine, leaves rustling, the birds chirping in the trees.

Brenna projected her message like a distress signal. She kept it simple: *Help us. Need help.*

She felt the nearby crows answer first. She opened her eyes and watched as they flew from the trees, abandoning their nests, breaking off their relentless search for food. Like a distant cloud they flocked together, skimming the treetops, heading in her direction.

Help us. Bad men. Find them. Stop them. Brenna repeated. She was careful not to overdo it. Animals killed for food or to protect themselves and their young. Killing for the sake of killing went against their natural instincts. Asking them to do so would break a Dyr'talara's connection with them, not to mention distort the natural balance of her magic.

Hrafn led the aerial attack. His black streak was followed by birds of different species: sparrows, thrushes, hawks, kites, even a large stork. Their wingbeats filled the air as they swooped overhead and then dove into the forest.

Shouts of surprise erupted. Twigs snapped. The sound of feet pounded through undergrowth in a vain attempt to get away as the birds set upon their targets.

Brenna risked peeking over the ramparts. Two men fled through the trees, tormented by a barrage of sharp talons and stinging beaks. One of them tripped, crying out for the other to stop and help him. He never did.

Brenna couldn't help but smile. *Puny indeed,* she thought to herself.

But how many more assassins lingered in the forest waiting to ambush them? She and Lothar had to get out of there.

Brenna wriggled her shield free from her shoulders and crawled to where Lothar cowered. "Let's go," she said.

The prince refused to move.

"If you don't get up, I'm leaving you here," she hissed.

The threat worked. He got up warily and followed her.

Crouching low, Brenna kept her shield and the wall's crenelles between her and the forest. Lothar kept pace beside her. With any luck, they could reach Midgard before the assassins had a chance to catch up with them. There was no doubt in Brenna's mind that the ambush was linked to her investigation into the wall's breach. Apparently, the traitor had friends, friends willing to kill her and the future king of Midgard to keep his identity a secret. But without tracing the magical fingerprint that corrupted the wall, Brenna had no hope of discovering who the traitor was. So why attack them? Lothar mentioned they were ambushed by Frost Giants too. Did that have something to do with this? Were the ambushes related?

"Who conjured the bifrost that brought you to Baldersted?" Brenna asked.

The prince hesitated. "I did, but…" He paused.

"But what?"

"The bifrost spat us out faomrs from Baldersted—a lot farther than I crafted it to."

"What do you think happened?"

The prince shrugged. "I don't know. It was almost as if…" His voice trailed off. "As if someone had tampered with the bifrost's magic too."

Two instances of tampering? Midgard's walls and now the bifrost—was there a connection?

These can't be coincidences, Brenna thought. "Who was at the bifrost to see you off yesterday?"

"Haakon and Loremaster Onem."

"Were you the first one there?"

"No, you were there...I mean, Hel who was shapeshifted as you, and—" Lothar stopped running. He looked at her; his round face had grown pale.

Brenna stepped closer. "Hel and who else?" she asked.

The prince swallowed. "Hel and Onem were there first."

Brenna swallowed. Could it be? Their own Loremaster?

The puzzle pieces fell into place. Onem had the money and influence to hire assassins, and a Loremaster could've made short work of the wall's defenses to let Hel into the city.

Onem was their prime suspect...if not the actual traitor. Brenna was sure of it.

"We have to get to my father and tell him everything," she said.

"Brenna!" Lothar slowed and pointed to five Vikings coming up the ramparts.

Brenna's throat clenched. By the way they were dressed, she could tell they weren't Wall Guards. *Were they more assassins, coming to finish the job?*

She was about to grab Lothar and turn back uphill when she recognized one of the burly men. He was large, with a black beard, and wearing a bearskin draped over his shoulders.

"Haakon! Thank Odin it's you." Brenna ran to him and, despite herself, threw her arms around the Jarl's ample belly.

"Are you two all right?" he asked.

"Better now that you're here," she said.

Did he know we were being attacked? Did he track the assassins up here, to the Pillar of Halvor?

It didn't matter. Everything would be okay now. Even if the assassins managed to escape their clash with the forest animals, they wouldn't dare mount another attack with Haakon and four warriors present. She and Lothar were safe. Brenna could tell him everything, confront Loremaster Onem, see what the old warlock had to say about the evidence she'd found. She buried her face deeper into the Jarl's bearskin.

That's when she smelled it. An acrid and sour smell. It had a sharp, pungent, metallic flavor…almost like brimstone. It matched the odor she smelled a half hour ago where the wall had been breached. She remembered smelling something similar when she entered the Loremaster's lab yesterday. She dismissed it as another foul stench coming from one of Onem's nasty jars. It had actually come from Haakon. His pelt reeked of it.

But Haakon has no magic, how did he…

The horizontal markings on the Pillar.

Brenna thought they could have been manmade. Were they grooves meant to insert gunpowder into the rock? So neither erosion nor magic exposed the iron deposits. Gunpowder—maybe dynamite—was used, and the blast had left its residue on the traitor.

And how did Haakon know we were up here?

Brenna felt a wave of dizziness. She pushed away from the Jarl. Something in her eyes betrayed her thoughts. Anger mixed with shock and fear.

Haakon thrust out a calloused hand. It clamped around Brenna's throat, squeezing her windpipe. One of his Viking henchmen rushed forward and pulled the sword from her scabbard.

"Let me go," Brenna rasped. She grabbed Haakon's wrist, struggling to break his grip.

"What are you doing?" Lothar said, stepping toward them. "Unhand her or I'll—"

The Jarl lashed out, smacking Lothar with a vicious backhand. The impact sent the prince spinning to the ground.

Haakon focused Brenna with a fierce gaze. "You couldn't leave well enough alone, could you?" he growled.

"Why are you doing this?" she managed through the choke-hold.

"It's nothing personal, Brenna. It was all supposed to end in the avalanche. It was supposed to look like an accident."

"But I wasn't even there during the avalanche." She'd already been handed over to the Hex at that point. Haakon must have known that.

His yellow-stained teeth smiled under his prickly, black beard. "You weren't the target."

What was he talking about? If she'd been delivered to the Hex, and the Hexhunter was to be captured alive, who else could be the target? Sarah?

That doesn't make sense either. There's no reason for Haakon to kill her.

That only left—

Hrodi! she cursed.

Brenna squirmed and twisted in Haakon's grip. "Lothar! Run! Get out of here!"

Still on the ground, the prince held a hand tenderly to his split lip. He scrambled to his feet, but before he could get away, the henchman who had taken her sword grabbed Lothar from behind.

"Do it," Haakon ordered.

Without hesitation, the Viking thrust Brenna's sword through the prince's back.

"No!" Brenna cried.

Eyes wide, Lothar peered down where the sword tip, smeared crimson red, poked from his chest. A feeble groan escaped his lips. Then his eyes rolled back and he dropped dead onto the cobble-stones.

All Brenna could do was stare at his crumpled body. Blood bloomed through his tunic. It pooled under him, spilling between the cobblestones in little rivulets. Lothar had been a pompous jerk for most of his life, but he didn't deserve to die…not like this.

Tears streamed down Brenna's cheeks. She focused her rage on Haakon. "You filthy *gargan*! Why would you betray us?"

"That was the deal I made with the Death Queen," he said. He didn't seem bothered in the slightest at ordering Lothar's cold-blooded murder. "Hel needed a way to get to the Hexhunter," he went on, "and I needed the heir of Midgard to die." He pulled her closer so they were face to face. Brenna saw a flicker of madness in his eyes. "Can you imagine they were going to replace me with this pompous whelp? I don't think so. No member of House Ericson is fit to rule our Folklore. But *I am*. I've done so for over a decade. I will make Midgard great again."

Brenna looked at him, disgusted.

Power had been his motive. He'd gotten a taste of real power and was unwilling to give it up. But he *was* willing to sacrifice the welfare of Midgard, her home, to do it.

"You won't get away with this," she croaked. The threat sounded hollow, pathetic, coming out hoarse and barely audible.

Haakon's nostrils flared like an angry bull. "I *will* get away with it," he said. "Lothar was supposed to die on the mission to Baldersted, but Hel never followed through on our deal. Lothar was allowed to live. I didn't think would have another chance to kill him…until this morning. My spies told me he had followed you up here. Things couldn't have worked out better. As it turns out, the people will learn that *you* murdered the prince in a fit of rage. Everyone knows of your temper, Brenna, *and* we saw how angry you were at Lothar during our meeting. Unfortunately, I didn't reach you in time before you drove your sword into the prince's back." His eyes grew hard as stone. "But I was able to kill you before you escaped."

Haakon squeezed, ready to crush her windpipe, when a rush of black feathers overwhelmed him. Crows, dozens of them, descended on the traitor and his men, circling and attacking like a maelstrom of angry claws and jabbing beaks. In an effort to protect his face from the onslaught, Haakon let Brenna go. She collapsed onto the cobblestones, gasping for breath. Spots darted in front of her eyes. She tried to stand, but couldn't get her legs to work.

Brenna dragged herself on the cobblestoned rampart instead, inching away from the treacherous Jarl and closer to the wall's edge.

Looking back, she picked out Hrafn in the feathered turmoil. He'd seen her in trouble and took it upon himself to rally his flock.

Haakon thrashed his bulky arms like a frenzied berserker. Several crows were knocked to the ground, causing some of them to break off their attack or meet the same fate as their injured comrades.

Free of birds for the moment, Haakon spied Brenna trying to get away. He stomped toward her.

Brenna couldn't let herself be caught again. It would be over if she did. Haakon was going to blame her for Lothar's murder. She wasn't going to give the traitor the satisfaction of parading her body through Midgard's streets. She glanced at her sword impaled in the prince's body. Lothar's eyes stared lifeless into the sky.

She reached the edge of the ramparts. Looking over the wall, she saw the full might of Idun Falls crashing in a powerful display of water, rocks, and mist three hundred feet below.

"I'm going to tear you limb from limb!" Haakon snarled.

Brenna closed her eyes, said a small prayer, and before the Jarl could grab her, rolled off the edge.

Chapter 45

Grayle flopped on deck, battered and exhausted. Sarah lay on her stomach next to him. Their tangled bodies were drenched, thrashed, and bruised inside the netting that hauled them aboard. But the pain no longer mattered.

Shutting his eyes, Grayle tried to piece together what he'd seen while under the runestone's power—his birth, his parents, their betrayal. Ever since he turned up in Vancouver's Stanley Park, his singular goal had been to find out where he came from. That goal—the dream—of being reunited with his family had sustained him through difficult times. All that had been shattered in a moment. He had survived a duel with Hel, two Hel-hounds, being chased by Frost Giants, Crossers, an enormous snake, and a booby-trapped tomb. And what was his reward? The knowledge that he'd be an orphan for the rest of his life. Everything he'd been through in the last few days seemed pointless now.

"Get off yer duffs an' gimme a hand!" Grigsby shouted from the rudder.

Grayle and Sarah twisted out of the netting. They ran to the *Drakkar's* stern.

The lead Roman flagship raced at them like a speedboat, churning whitewater as it cut through the water. Oars dropped in and out of the water like the legs of a centipede crawling across the Golden Horn estuary. The vessel's painted eyes and twelve-foot ram plowing above the waterline added to its lethal appearance. The ship's captain stood on the bridge near the prow, dressed in blood-red scarlet, helmet tucked under his arm. Even from this distance, Grayle could see his cocky smile.

"Can't we go any faster?" Grayle shouted.

The Caretaker steered around a massive container ship crossing the harbor. "We gotta get past the buoys first. Once we reach open water, we may have a chance."

The buoys—the magical barrier controlling Folklorian ship speeds.

Grayle scanned the horizon. He could make out the red markers bobbing in the water a mile away. Judging by the rate the triremes were gaining on the *Drakkar*, they'd be overtaken long before reaching the buoys.

He and Sarah stared helplessly as the flagship armed its forward ballista. Two soldiers cranked a winch lever, forcing tension into the bowstring, while another Roman slid an eight-foot arrow into the oversized crossbow's groove. A third soldier tied a rope to the base of the jagged arrowhead.

"They want to harpoon us like a whale—stop us from escaping," Grayle said.

The weapon swivelled in their direction.

"Can't let one of those hit us," Sarah warned.

"Can you deflect it with your shield?"

She looked at him, open-mouthed. "That's an eight-foot arrow with an iron spike. No, I can't *deflect* it."

Over the wind and lashing water, they heard the Roman captain shout, "Ignis!"

The ballista's arrow shot like a missile.

"Hard to port!" Grayle yelled, not even sure which direction port was.

The *Drakkar* veered left.

The arrow overshot its target, slicing into the water twenty yards off their starboard. But the rope attached to it crossed the *Drakkar's* deck. The rope went taut as the ship's forward motion dragged it along both railings, grinding into the wood.

"Watch out!" Sarah shouted.

She and Grayle hit the deck. Grigsby did the same, leaving the rudder unmanned as the rope scraped above their heads. It hooked onto the *Drakkar's* sternpost, causing the longship to lurch and slow to a crawl.

Grayle scrambled to his feet and rushed aft. He took out the Emerald Dagger and freed the bloodstained blade from its gold scabbard. He sawed at the rope tethering them to the trireme. The sternpost's wooden strakes creaked and snapped under the rope's pressure.

By the time Sarah joined him, the triremes had shortened the distance between them by another twenty yards. More arrows were being loaded into the ballistas, ready to fire.

"Don't you have any water spells or something?" Grayle asked, busy sawing away.

Sarah bit her lip and shook her head.

"In a thousand years, you never thought about adding an outboard or some cannons to this thing?"

"Cannons. That's it! Grayle, you're a genius. Stop cutting."

"But I almost got it!"

"No! Keep us tethered."

"Are you crazy? Why?"

"We need to keep them close. Grigs, throw me your bandolier."

With one hand still on the rudder, the elf unbuckled a leather strap hidden under his duster. Attached to the strap were four metal orbs, the same Grayle had seen him tossing outside the Topkapi Palace.

Grayle slid the dagger back into its scabbard. "What are you planning on doing? Playing catch with the Romans?"

"Come here." Sarah threw him the bandolier. "Throw one of these in the air when I tell you to."

Grayle caught the strap and unhooked one of the metal orbs. It was the size of a softball but weighed as much as a six-pound shot put he'd used in gym class. He felt the intricate metal designs carved on its surface.

Sarah stood back and spread her arms. Despite the sunlight, the familiar shimmering blue of her magic charged her hands. What she was going to do was anyone's guess.

"Flip the switch," she shouted.

What switch? Grayle turned the device in his hand and found a tiny lever between the carvings. He flicked it up. "What is this thing anyway?" he asked.

"It's a bomb."

"A bomb!"

He juggled the orb between his hands like a hot potato.

"Throw it in the air, genius!"

Grayle flung it.

"Vanya!"

Sarah pulsed the metal cylinder, shooting it over the water like a cannonball. It landed with a metallic clunk on the flagship's deck.

The Romans scrambled, either trying to pick up the bomb or run away from it.

A boom swept across the deck. The concussive force flattened waves on the water's surface. At the same time, Grayle watched

Romans collapse like bowling pins. Some fell into the hold where the oarsmen sat. Those too close to ship's edge toppled overboard.

"Again!" Sarah shouted, changing position to get a better aim at the second trireme. It sailed parallel to the flagship.

Grayle unhooked another cylinder, flipped the switch, and tossed it in the air.

"Vanya!"

The flash bomb soared, landing on the second trireme's bow. It bounced across their deck and disappeared into the hold.

Whomp!

Oars on the trireme's portside stopped rowing. The ship veered hard to the left. The soldiers still conscious on the flagship waved frantically, trying to keep the other vessel from colliding into them. It was no use. Half their rowers were knocked out. There was no one left on the ship's deck to see their panicked waves or hear their shouts. The collision almost happened in slow motion. The second ship smashed into the flagship's oars first. They snapped like chopsticks, splintering into the sea. Then, with a crack of a hundred wooden strakes, the ram pierced the flagship's hull. A hole the size of a bus tore into its flank. The force of the collision severed the ropes securing its mainsail. The mast cracked and keeled onto the deck, crushing anyone caught underneath. Those Romans still conscious dove overboard, abandoning their ships.

"Now, Grayle!" Sarah shouted. "Cut the rope!"

He dropped the bandolier and rushed to the sternpost. The rope had carved into the strakes, leaving a gash of stripped wood. He worked the Dagger's blade furiously back and forth. With a satisfying snap, the final threads split apart.

The *Drakkar* accelerated, cutting through the choppy water. The red buoys passed by on their left.

"*Drakkar,* get us the heck outta here! Full speed," Grigsby shouted.

The longship's sail caught wind and, free of the barrier's magic, rocketed across the Sea of Marmara.

Chapter 46

A half hour passed before Sarah forced herself from the *Drakkar's* stern. She'd been scanning the horizon for Roman ships on a pursuit course. Nothing so far. If they were being followed, there would've been a sign by now.

Despite overwhelming odds, they had escaped Istanbul with a piece of Mimir's Stone. They didn't, however, escape unscathed. Grayle had retreated into himself again, leaning over the starboard railing, gazing out at the sea. He hadn't moved or uttered a word since their escape.

Sarah groped for her pink bag pushed against the portside railing. It was drenched, the laptop inside probably wrecked. Opening the front flap, she dug her hand inside and exhaled as her fingers found what she was searching for. She pulled out the miniaturized runestone and held it up between her thumb and index finger.

"Is that what I think it is?" Grigs asked.

Sarah nodded.

The elf tended to the longship's rudder even though the *Drakkar* was on auto-pilot. His Adam's apple bobbed. "Let's have a look at it."

Wary of where Grayle was standing, Sarah enlarged the runestone back to its original size. He'd been drawn to the runestone earlier, unable to control his actions. She didn't want the same thing happening again.

"It matches the piece we found in the Vancouver Museum." She brought up the picture on her phone and held it to the fragment lying on the ship's deck. Like two pieces of a puzzle, the top and bottom ends aligned perfectly.

> *The All-Father's eye waits in caverns deep,*
> *Under crescent moon it rests in sleep,*
> *Destiny favors those who heed*
> *To stop Ragnarok*
> *An Auralex must*
> *Battling*
> ***By threat of death***
> ***In a Hexhunter's hands***
> ***Will truth reveal***
> ***Others can***

"In a Hexhunter's hands," Grigs grumbled. "What the heck is that supposed to mean?"

Sarah had no clue. She was shocked when the stone's translation first appeared on her screen back in the chasm. But the mere mention of an Auralex *and* a Hexhunter on Mimir's Stone proved there was a connection between them and finding the Eye. Sarah debated whether to tell Grigs about what happened in the Tomb. Grayle's reaction to the runestone was unlike anything she'd seen or heard of before. It had consumed him, taken over his body.

"Well...whatever the case, we can stop now," Grigsby said when she didn't answer. "We have a fragment of Mimir's Stone.

Without all the markers, I doubt Hel, Caine, or anyone'll be able to get their hands on the Eye of Odin. We can bring our piece to the Vikings for safekeepin' an' be done with this whole thing."

Be done with the whole mission? Could it be that simple?

Sarah might have agreed with him had her dead mother not made a ghostly appearance. More was riding on getting the Eye now than ever before. Her mother's future hung in the balance, as odd as that sounded. Generally, the dead had no future.

But if there's even the slightest chance I can return Mum to the world of the living, don't I have to try? Isn't that what a good daughter would do?

"While we're at it," Grigs added, keeping his voice low, "we should hand over the Hexhunter to the Coven too. I reckon all will be forgiven once you do. Things can finally get back to the way they were."

"How can you say that?" Sarah shot back. "We've gotten this far because of him, and now you want to turn him over, just like that?"

"Whaddya suggest we do, adopt him? The mission's over."

"It's not over. Look at what the runestone says! It mentions an Auralex and Hexhunter by name. He and I are a part of this."

"But you ain't sure what the other halves say. They could warn us the kid's the doom of us all!"

Sarah didn't believe that. "It could also say he'll save us all," she countered.

Would Halfdan go through all the trouble of designing clues, traps, and puzzles only to have one betray the other in the end?

The elf huffed. "In a pig's eye he'll save us."

"*Pig-headed* is more like it…as in that's what you are for never giving him a chance." Sarah had to get away from him, which was tough to do when stuck on a boat. She minimized the stone, stuffed it back into her bag, and got up. "Things will never be back to the way they were," she muttered and trudged to where Grayle stood.

He was staring at the passing whitecaps.

How much of the conversation did he overhear?

She gave him a sidelong glance. Water dripped from his nose. Or were those tears?

The last few hours had taken their toll on him, both physically and emotionally. He looked as if he had been in a fistfight. There were a number of small cuts and bruises on his forehead and right cheek. Sarah was more worried about the scars she couldn't see.

"I saw them," he whispered, wiping his nose with the back of his hand.

"Saw who?" Sarah asked gently. He had to be talking about his experience while under the runestone's influence. She remembered what had happened to him. "Grayle, back in the chasm, after you touched the stone, you had an aura. I could see it for the first time. I could feel what you were feeling." The longer he was in contact with it, the darker his emotions became. His excitement had turned to confusion and despair. Then anger.

Not just anger—hatred.

"Who did you see?" Sarah asked.

Grayle swallowed. "My-my parents."

"Your parents?"

How was that possible? Was the runestone a conduit of some kind, able to draw on the Eye of Odin's power to see into the past? That would be too incredible…and dangerous. Level Five artifacts were unpredictable at best; the extent of their powers was largely unknown. The same was true for the Eye and its markers. Sarah couldn't be sure how the runestone would affect Grayle. Did it matter? Whatever happened *did* happen, and the experience had shaken him to the core.

"I saw my birth," he went on. "There were others in the room. Folklore agents came and…" Grayle paused.

Sarah wanted to hug him, do something, say anything that would make him feel better. But she couldn't fix his past any more than she could fix her own.

"Is there anything I can do?" She reached over and brushed the damp hair from his forehead, before resting her hand on his shoulder.

He shrugged it off. "I'm fine. It's no big deal."

"Grayle, it *is* a big deal. You saw your parents. That's what you've been looking for—"

"They didn't want me!"

"What?"

"They didn't want me, okay. Is that what you wanted to hear? Where did the Hexhunter come from? He came from a family who wanted him dead. The woman in the feathered cloak was supposed to kill me, but she didn't. Why?"

What's he talking about? What woman in a feathered cloak?

Sarah was about to ask what he meant when the *Drakkar* lurched to a hard stop. Both she and Grayle grabbed onto the railing to keep from falling over.

"We have company!" Grigsby yelled.

Sarah's heart jumped. She rushed to the bow with Grayle close behind.

Ten ships, smaller than the Roman triremes but looking just as fierce, blocked their path. Sarah recognized the giant reversed black V's stitched onto their red sails.

Oh no.

"How'd the Romans get ahead of us?" Grayle asked, his bitterness seemed forgotten for the moment.

"They're Greek, not Roman," Sarah said. "Spartan, to be exact."

"So they're Spartan. That's okay, isn't it?"

Grigsby came up next to them. "They must've bin waitin' for us. Heard you were in the area. I reckon they're aimin' to settle the score 'bout the helmet incident."

"What *helmet incident*?" Grayle asked.

The elf ignored him. He reached for his Winchester. "Should we fight our way outta this?"

"Not much we can do against ten triremes," Sarah replied nervously. She could only watch as the enemy ships surrounded them. "Can we outrun them?"

The *Drakkar* creaked and groaned.

That sounded like a no.

A Greek soldier balanced on the bow rail of the nearest ship. His bronze shin greaves gleamed in the sunlight, and a red cape fluttered over his left shoulder.

"Sarah Finn!" he called out. "By order of King Leonidas, you are under arrest."

"Who's King Leonidas? What's. Going. *On*?" Grayle asked, getting more frustrated.

"Drop your sail, surrender your vessel, and prepare to be boarded," the soldier ordered. "Any resistance will be met with extreme force."

"What do we do?" Grigs asked.

Sarah had no idea. They couldn't escape; they couldn't fight. There was only one thing they could do.

She pursed her lips. "Signal our surrender."

Epilogue

The cowering figure scuttled like an insect from one shadow to the next. Her footsteps cautiously approached the Tomb of Serpents. She didn't care much for the potential riches inside. Her goal was something more precious than the prospect of claiming a piece of Mimir's Stone. She needed to satiate a hunger—one that had fuelled her need to follow the young witch and Hexhunter from the far north to this dismal place.

She skittered from the cover of one stone to the next, nervously scanning her surroundings before creeping closer to the tomb door.

She'd been here before, over a millennia ago. She was left for dead by that cursed Halfdan, back when she was a powerful witch. She'd forgotten her name.

Was it Atla? Astrid? Maybe Alviss?

Her memories were clouded, as though they belonged to another person in a different time.

She caught the faintest scent of copper and iron.

Blood.

Her pupils dilated and mouth watered.

For a moment she was so consumed by the hunger, she ignored her cautious nature and wanted to run to the scent's origin, lap it up without a care as to who might be watching. It was like she could hardly control her actions, an addiction that consumed her every waking moment, inhabited her dreams and nightmares at night, ever since she found out about *his* existence.

She forced herself to calm. Her stomach growled like a suffering animal, but she resisted dashing toward the source of the scent. She didn't survive a thousand years by being reckless and stupid.

Ten more yards.

She knew the Hexhunter was no longer in the vicinity, but his scent lingered.

With three more scuttles, keeping to the stretching shadows, she arrived at the entrance.

There. Smeared in crimson streaks along the door's edge was his blood.

This is where he must have pried it open.

She couldn't contain herself any longer. She braced the door with both hands, unhinged her jaw, and allowed her tongue to taste the precious blood. Her body shivered as soon as she swallowed. She could feel its energy like a spark of electricity, charging every magical molecule in her withered body. The potency his blood possessed would sustain her for another century at least, increasing her powers tenfold.

But her hunger wasn't satisfied. It only grew worse. The few droplets served as the barest of appetizers.

She needed the main course.

And now that she had a taste, nothing was going to stop her from getting it.

Coming Fall 2018

The Raiders of Folklore: Book Three
THE PRISONERS OF SPARTA

Acknowledgments

Again, I would like to start by acknowledging YOU, the reader, for finishing my second book. Your kind encouragement and enthusiasm for my stories keeps me going. Thank you.

But I would be lost without the family, friends, cat (yes, I said *cat*), and professionals supporting me.

Big thanks to Ian and Patricia Robertson, John and Erin Weninger, Luke Corrigan, Rino Cinel, Christine McCauley, and many others (sorry if I didn't mention you by name) for your help and ongoing belief in my projects. To Pintado, for a stunning cover. To Jennifer Pendergast, for her illustration of yet another piece of Mimir's Stone (two more to go...if Grayle and Sarah survive). To Kate at Teen Eyes Editorial, for her editing expertise. To J.R.R. Tolkien, whose Sindarin Elvish language forms the basis of Sarah's magical incantations. To the gang at Hilliside Starbucks for keeping my fuel gauge at full. Strangely enough (or maybe not so strange), I'd like to thank my cat, Dopey, for lying on my keyboard, sprawling over my paper drafts, and perching upon my hunched shoulders when I needed a break. To my parents, Udo and Kirsten, not enough can be said about what you've done for me. And last but not least, to Shannon—none of this would mean anything without you.

About the Author

Dennis Staginnus dreamed of becoming an archaeologist, an intergalactic smuggler, or a covert operative. He became a teacher and librarian instead, at least until the CIA calls or he's abducted by aliens. He's the author of THE EYE OF ODIN and THE EMERALD DAGGER, the first two books in THE RAIDERS OF FOLKLORE series. He lives in British Columbia, Canada, with his wife and a clowder of black cats.

For more information, visit:
www.dennisstaginnus.com

CPSIA information can be obtained
at www.ICGtesting.com
Printed in the USA
LVOW13s1741290517
536187LV00010B/488/P

9 780993 682483